MARKED

HOSTAGE RESCUE TEAM SERIES

KAYLEA CROSS

MARKED

Copyright © 2014
by Kaylea Cross

* * * * *

Cover Art & Formatting by
<u>Sweet 'N Spicy Designs</u>

* * * * *

ISBN: 978-1499649895

Dedication

This story is meant as a salute to the brave and extremely dedicated men who serve in the FBI's Hostage Rescue Team. They stand ready to act in a wide variety of operations both at home and abroad, and for that they deserve our heartfelt gratitude.

More specifically, I'd like to dedicate this book to my late beta reader, author Julieanne Reeves, who passed away suddenly and unexpectedly a few weeks ago at the far too young age of forty, leaving behind two children. She always went above and beyond for me, checking all my details with her military and law enforcement contacts. I hope you'll consider reading her romantic suspense title, Razing Kayne.

Thank you, Julie, for your sweet and giving nature, your attention to detail and the support you always gave to the romance community. You were taken from us far too soon. May you rest in peace, and may God hold your precious babies in the palm of His hand.

Kaylea

Author's Note

You first met FBI Special Agent Jake Evers in the Titanium Security Series, and because many of you asked for it, here he is in his own story, kicking off the Hostage Rescue Team Series.

Each book will feature a different hero from my imagination who serves in the FBI's fabled HRT, and I'm so looking forward to you meeting these brave and dedicated men. I hope you enjoy their stories and that you learn something about these incredible guys!

Happy reading!

Kaylea Cross

Prologue

Servare Vitas (To Save Lives)
-FBI Hostage Rescue Team motto

Seated in the back of a tactical truck, Special Agent Jake Evers took a good-natured punch to the arm from one of his teammates without flinching.

"Good to have you back, farmboy. I've missed you," Tuck said in his southern-Alabama drawl as he sat next to him on one of the benches built into the back along one side. "Been a while since you graced us with your presence on an op. Think you remember the ropes around here after all your vacay time?"

Vacay, ha. "Pretty sure I do." He'd missed the guys too but he hadn't been gone *that* long. Only around three weeks this time, overseas again with a handpicked paramilitary team led by the NSA's legendary Alex Rycroft. Something in Jake's background as a Captain with the 75th Ranger Regiment and his other credentials must have impressed Rycroft, because Jake had gotten a tap from his superiors months ago and he'd been on loan to the team off and on over the past few months. After months of hunting they'd finally tracked down and killed the notorious terrorist mastermind Malik Hassani, in Pakistan.

Tuck adjusted his gear as he spoke. "That's good to hear, wouldn't want you to be rusty. You learn any new tricks over there?"

"Maybe. You'll just have to wait and find out." That chemical threat at the end with Hassani had been scary as shit. Training for it and actually dealing with it firsthand were two very different things. The entire team had been tested and treated for sarin exposure. He'd been lucky not to have suffered direct exposure, but it was an experience he never wanted to repeat again. On the upside, it had sure made him see things clearly though.

It had made him think a lot about Rachel, and the mistakes he'd made with her. While getting checked out at the hospital after the sarin scare he'd made up his mind to track her down the first chance he got when he returned to Virginia. Before he could get to it, his team had been sent down here to Miami. Just another day in the life of an FBI Hostage Rescue Team member.

He pulled his balaclava on, the unseasonably muggy late October night air reminding him a little of Karachi. He'd only arrived back in D.C. two days ago and he was still adjusting to the time difference when they'd flown to Miami this afternoon. But there was nothing like an op to get the blood pumping and cure a case of jetlag.

The rest of the team loaded up and Clay Bauer slammed the back doors shut, enveloping them in near darkness. Up front the driver put the big vehicle in gear and steered away from the warehouse they'd used as a staging area.

Jake and the others checked their weapons and

comms on the way to the target. He'd rejoined his team near the end of their one-hundred-twenty day operations cycle. Currently they were on their way to a major drug runner's compound to help out a DEA FAST team with a warrant, search and seizure, and hopefully some arrests.

They were acting on fresh intel that placed the drug runner and two of his deputies at the home in south Miami. The place was heavily fortified and surveillance video showed there were armed guards crawling all over the grounds. This op was definitely going to be all about shock and awe in an effort to reduce the chances of taking large amounts of direct fire. They'd planned this carefully, leaving nothing to chance, and hopefully when all was said and done he and all his teammates would be flying back to Quantico within the next few hours minus any bullet holes.

The six minute drive went by fast. All the guys were silent as they drove the last few miles to the target, each focused on what they had to do. Jake ran through the plan, the contingencies and emergency protocol in case something went sideways—because something usually did on an op like this. The truck slowed as it reached the dropoff point. Jake rose with the others and faced the rear doors. Over the radio the FAST team reported they were in place; everyone was ready to rock.

Cradling his M4 in front of him, pulse slow and steady as he waited for the team leader to open the back doors, Rachel's face flashed through Jake's mind. Pale golden skin, dark brown hair and warm hazel eyes.

Shit, he had to find her after this was over. He just hoped it wasn't too late, that she hadn't moved on for good.

The team leader threw the doors open and everyone poured out. Faint light from the compound spotlights illuminated the dense brush ahead of them. They were going to skirt it and enter at the most vulnerable point along the fence line.

Poised in line with the others as they crept toward their target, Jake locked down all thoughts of the woman he'd let slip through his fingers and got ready to do his part in unleashing hell on the men inside the compound.

Chapter One

Six months later

Rachel Granger swung her condo door open and stilled when she heard the rumble of male voices coming from the living room.

Great.

A wave of exhaustion rolled over her as she realized her brother, who was staying the weekend with her as he sometimes did, had brought friends home with him from college. Normally she didn't mind if he brought people over without asking because she wanted him to feel at home in her place, but it was seven o'clock on a Friday night. After a long week of working overtime at Edge Architectural Firm all she wanted was a hot bath, a pizza delivery, and some peace and quiet with which to enjoy them both.

Get over it. Enjoy your time with your brother. She shut the door, put her shoes and jacket in the entryway closet and set her briefcase on top of the granite countertop in the kitchen.

"Brandon? I'm home."

The voices quieted and a few seconds later her brother emerged from around the corner. Tall and slender with hazel eyes and features that only hinted at their half-Chinese ancestry, he looked seventeen instead of twenty, and she still had to remind herself that he was all grown up.

"Hey. Some of the guys wanted to come over and hang out. Hope that's okay."

She put on a smile, pushing aside her exhaustion. "It's fine. Who is it?"

His posture stiffened slightly, a wary expression entering his eyes. "The usual guys."

She arched a brow, aware of the tendrils of dread tightening her stomach. "And Tim?"

"Yeah. I didn't think you'd be home until later." Now he looked almost guilty, which he should.

Not wanting to get into a confrontation over it, Rachel turned away and opened the fridge to pull out a bottle of orange juice and take a moment to compose herself. Brandon knew how she felt about Tim and how she felt about him being in her home; she'd made it extremely clear the last time he'd been over when she'd overheard some of the whacked shit he'd been saying to Brandon and the others. Apparently her eternally optimistic brother was hoping she'd change her mind about him.

Not likely. "You hungry?" she asked over her shoulder instead.

His face brightened, as though he assumed she'd caved and let the matter drop for good. Again, not happening. She had every intention of talking about it once Tim left.

"I could eat. You wanna order something in? We'll all pitch in."

"Sure." Not that she planned to eat with them if Tim was here, but she could be civil and wait until everyone left before making it absolutely *crystal* clear this time that Brandon was never to bring him here again.

She chugged half the bottle of juice and turned back to face him just as two of Brandon's friends and Tim stepped into the room. Tim's dark gaze immediately zeroed in on her, something about it too keen, too focused. Not in a sexual way, exactly, but the gleam in his eyes still sent a shiver of unease through her. His mixed features spoke of South Asian or maybe Eurasian blood in addition to Chinese. He'd only recently come to the U.S. from China and started hanging around Brandon's circle of friends from college, much to her chagrin.

"Hi, Rachel," he said to her in a heavily accented voice, the warmth in his smile not quite reaching his eyes.

"Hi," she answered quietly, then dismissed him by looking at the others. She opened her mouth to ask them about dinner but Tim interrupted her.

"How's your work going?" he asked in Mandarin, reluctantly drawing her attention back to him.

"Fine," she responded in the same language then focused on Brandon. On top of creepy, Tim was rude to speak Mandarin in front of the two others who couldn't. She shot her brother a hard look that said: *I can't believe you brought* him *here again.*

"I'm gonna go change. You guys order what you want and I'll pay for my portion." She didn't miss the frown or the pleading look her brother sent her at her words of dismissal. Ignoring both, she pushed past the young men and headed down the cream-tiled hallway to her room at the back of the spacious condo, aware of the tingling between her shoulder blades that told her Tim was still watching her until she disappeared from view.

As she passed by the guest room door she saw that

Brandon already had his stuff set on the bed, but she paused when she noticed her Mac laptop sitting open on the desk with the screen on. She'd left it closed and password locked before work that morning, and the only other person who knew her password was Brandon. The voices she'd heard when she'd walked in the door had come from this room. Which meant Tim had been in here.

A wave of annoyance rose inside her. The last time Brandon had brought Tim over, rather than hang out with their buddies, Tim had stood behind her in here watching her work until she'd been forced to close the laptop and confront him in order to stop his snooping. Instead of apologizing and backing off, he'd followed her back into the kitchen, asking prying questions about her job and what she was currently working on, what buildings she'd helped design in the area.

At first she'd thought he might have a crush on her and maybe that was his way of hitting on her, but that wasn't it. She wasn't sure if he was mentally ill or not, but she knew she wanted nothing to do with him.

Already suspicious that he might have been in here snooping some more, she went over and refreshed the screen. A document relating to one of her most recent projects appeared. Her lips thinned in irritation.

Quiet footsteps approached from behind and then Brandon's voice reached her from the doorway. "He just wanted to see some more of your work."

Straightening, she whirled to face him and folded her arms across her chest, struggling to hold back the anger boiling up inside her. She didn't like the feel of this. Not at all. "Tim?"

Now her brother looked slightly apologetic. "Yeah. I didn't think you'd mind."

Seriously? "Well I *do* mind. I can't believe you'd let him into my laptop!"

She was outraged that Brandon would allow a relative stranger he *knew* she didn't like to violate her privacy this way, no matter how "interested" his buddy might seem to be in architecture. It wasn't like her brother to do something like that. They had a good relationship based on trust and respect, they rarely argued, and his behavior today shocked her. He was trying way too hard to fit in with the crowd and win Tim's approval, though why he'd want it in the first place she'd never understand.

"What the hell, Brandon?"

He shifted his weight from one foot to the other and rubbed a hand over the back of his neck. "Sorry. He's just so interested in what you do, and he likes hanging around us because there's no language barrier. He told me he's thinking about switching into architecture too, after seeing some of your stuff."

She didn't care what Tim was thinking of choosing as a career path, he creeped her out with his too-intense stare, weird interest in her and her career, and the radical anti-government rhetoric she'd heard him spouting off about. And even without all that he had no business looking at her personal files.

She pushed out an annoyed breath, struggling to rein in her temper. As soon as this conversation was over with, she was kicking Tim out and she didn't care what her brother thought about it. "What else was he looking at?"

"I dunno. Jeez, would you calm down?"

"Uh, no, I *won't* calm down. Roles reversed, you'd freak if I let one of my friends look at your coding files for one of the video games you're developing."

Unable to curb her anger and resenting that his friends might be able to overhear them arguing, she gestured impatiently for Brandon to come in and close the door behind him. When he did she gave him a hard stare for a moment then shook her head as disappointment settled in her chest. "Again, why are you guys hanging around with someone like him?"

Brandon rolled his eyes, his sullen expression reminding her of a moody teenager. Which annoyed her even more. He was about to freaking graduate from college, not high school.

"I told you, he just transferred here from Beijing for the spring semester a few months ago, so he doesn't have many friends or anyone to hang out with. And he's not a bad guy if you'd just give him a chance and get to know him a little."

Her eyebrows shot upward at that. "Are you kidding me? Why would I want to get to know him? Have you not heard some of the things he's said?" And had he not noticed how weird Tim's behavior around her was?

"Whatever, he was only joking around."

She snorted. "Joking about terrorism and making stupid-ass comments about it isn't funny. I can't believe the others put up with him. Ray was totally embarrassed the last time Tim went off about how the U.S. government is 'the biggest terrorist organization on the planet and deserves whatever payback it gets'."

She shook her head again, letting him see her frustration, feeling like a parent scolding her child instead of a seven-years-older sister trying to make her brother see straight. Why wouldn't he listen to her warnings? Surely his internal radar was sharper than that. "Mom's paying for your degree and she sent you over here to study, not get mixed up with people who could get you into trouble. And if he's even half the hacker you say he is, he definitely could. You've got enough sense to know he's not someone you want your name to be linked with."

Brandon sighed and crossed his arms over his chest,

mimicking her stance as his expression closed up. "Are we done?"

His belligerent tone shocked her as much as it made her bristle. They'd had this same fight once before, with similar results. "No. I've told you before I don't want him here and—" She broke off when her gaze snagged on the laptop again, specifically on the empty slot on the side of it. She looked back at her brother, a sense of dread coiling in her gut. "Where's the flash drive that was plugged into this?"

He scowled at her, his expression turning militant. "I dunno, I didn't touch it."

"Well it's not there now." Her heart gave a little flutter of panic.

He shrugged. "You must have dropped it or something."

"I didn't drop it, Brandon," she snapped, crouching to scan the desk and floor.

When she didn't find it, Rachel turned her stare on her brother once again, her frustration and anxiety growing by the second. She had a feeling she knew exactly where it was. Dammit, her *work* files! "Go get it back from him. Right now, or I will." The hard look she gave him guaranteed that she was prepared to cause a scene if he didn't man up and take care of this himself.

Brandon narrowed his eyes in offense. "What, so because you don't like him Tim's automatically a thief now, too? Jesus, maybe you should take a look around first to make sure it's actually missing before you start accusing my friends of stealing stuff."

She sucked in a calming breath even as she frantically tried to remember exactly what she'd put on it. "It's not here, it's not on the desk or under it, and aside from you, he was the last person to have access to it."

Brandon snorted. "You're crazy. What the hell

would he want with your work files?"

"I don't know, but can you say for sure he *didn't* take them?" When her brother didn't answer, just continued to glare at her, she changed her tone and let him see how upset she was. "There were important documents on there. Designs and contracts, things confidential to our clients. Do you understand how much trouble I could be in?"

If she'd have thought her brother would bring his friends over and let them access her laptop, she never would have left it out in the open. But breaking client confidentiality wasn't what concerned her the most. Her instincts were screaming at her that something far more serious was potentially going on here. Tim's past behavior triggered too many internal alarms for her to ignore the warning.

"What if there *is* a reason he took them?" she continued when Brandon just stood there. "What if he's involved in something? Something illegal? He could be planning a robbery at one of the buildings and looking for the floor plans or something." She didn't trust Tim, hadn't from the first moment she'd met him, and she hadn't been shy about telling her brother so. Add in his extremist views, and hell yeah, she had every right to suspect he was up to no good.

Brandon shook his head, making a sound of disgust as though he couldn't believe what she was suggesting. "Screw this. You know what? I'll find somewhere else to stay on the weekends from now on so you won't have to deal with me or my fucked-up, criminal friends anymore." He stalked over to the bed and grabbed the duffel he'd placed at the foot.

She couldn't believe he would dare play the victim here, when she was the one whose privacy had been violated. "Come on! Brandon, just listen—"

"Forget it. I'm gone." He grabbed the bag and

slammed the guestroom door in her face when she tried to follow.

Fuming, she stared at the back of the white plastic door and forced herself to take a deep breath to keep from storming after him and continuing this fight with an audience. From the other room she heard Brandon telling the others they had to go. Making her the bad guy.

Just as she wrenched the door open to go after him, the front door shut with a resounding bang. Rachel sighed and pushed a hand through her shoulder-length hair, fighting to get a grip on her anger. Her brother was stubborn—even more stubborn than her, if that was possible—and if she went after him and confronted Tim in front of their friends she risked pushing him away even more.

The resounding silence in the suddenly empty condo was anything but peaceful. But at least now Tim was gone too.

You wanted the place to yourself and you got it. Careful what you wish for, Rachel.

"Perfect end to a perfect frigging week," she muttered, throwing open the door and marching down the hall to her room, unzipping her pencil skirt as she went. As she tossed her clothes in the laundry hamper, her cell phone rang. She glanced at the call display and groaned at the sight of her mother's number, calling from Shanghai.

There was only one thing she could say right now. *Hey, Mom. Brandon's being a little shit and I'm worried he's hanging with the wrong crowd, but he won't listen, and now one of his friends stole some of my work files. Brandon just took off in a huff and probably won't talk to me for the next week at least. So how's your day going?*

Yeah, that wasn't a conversation she was up to at

the moment. Deciding to call her mother back in the morning, she headed for the master bathroom for a much needed bubble bath in the hopes that it would help her unwind.

It didn't really help.

Later, while soaking in the tub, she mentally catalogued all the files she remembered being on that flash drive. She didn't think she'd lost anything vital, since all the files were saved on the firm's well-protected server at work, but she still felt violated and uneasy that someone had been digging into her work, let alone one of Brandon's friends.

She couldn't *prove* Tim had taken them, of course. All she had was knowing he'd been on her computer and a gut feeling that said he'd done it, plus the suspicion that something more was going on than she realized.

She sank deeper into the water, thinking about everything that had led up to this blowout with her brother. When he'd moved here from Beijing two years ago to finish his degree in computer sciences, Brandon had been desperate to fit in and make friends.

She'd never once told him he couldn't bring people here with him on the weekends when he'd wanted to get away from campus life. In her opinion he tried too hard to fit in, and his unflagging loyalty—one of the things she loved most about him—extended to even those "friends" who didn't deserve it. It drove her crazy to think that he could feel that insecure, but there was nothing she could do. She couldn't control the choices he made.

After the bath, she did a thorough search of her place and found yet another USB drive missing from her desk, this one also containing work files from some older projects a few years back. Just how the hell long had Tim been looking around in the guest room without supervision? Her bosses weren't going to be happy with her when she told them about this.

Furious, she tried calling her brother, then texting him. Of course she got no answer.

She paced the length of her condo, from the kitchen to her bedroom and back. Tim hadn't taken the flash drives for kicks, she knew it. Something on there must have interested him enough to warrant stealing it, but damned if she could figure it out.

Hours later, staring up at the patterns of light on her ceiling that seeped through her blinds from the streetlamps, she realized there was no way she was getting to sleep. Too upset about everything to shut her brain off, she got up a little after midnight and went into the living room to watch TV. She settled on a documentary about anti-terrorism operations involving the U.S., thinking of one man in particular from her past. Where was he now? Probably carrying out the same kinds of missions she was watching right now. When the show finished she picked up the remote, aimed it at the TV and had just started to press down on the power button when the FBI's Most Wanted list came on screen.

She almost dropped the remote when she saw Tim's picture for a split second. But too late. She'd already hit the button and the screen went dark. She jabbed the power button again, frantic to see the picture again, but when the screen came back to life the list was gone.

"Dammit," she muttered, then shut it down again and hurried to her laptop in the guestroom where she pulled up the FBI's website to look at the list.

Her eyes narrowed as she stared at the screen. Yep, she was ninety-five percent sure that was Tim. His hair was longer in this image, but the shape of the face and the mixed-Asian features were right.

Heart thudding, she searched for more information about him. Xang Xu, the name read beneath his picture. Wanted for computer fraud and various other cyber crimes. By the freaking FBI and god knew what other agencies.

Holy. Shit.

She shot up from the couch and rushed to the bedroom to grab her cell. Then she hesitated.

Didn't matter that it was the middle of the night. Brandon was too mad to answer her call right now and she was pretty sure if he did, she wouldn't get to the part that "Tim" was wanted by the FBI before he hung up. She tried calling anyway, got no answer, and rather than leave a voicemail she sent a text.

I know you're mad, but call me right away! Got something important to tell you.

She thought about calling the cops too, but on the off chance she was wrong about that picture being "Tim", there was only one person she could think of to go to with her suspicions. Only one person she was comfortable sharing this with.

A mixture of nerves and butterflies buzzed in her stomach at the thought of re-establishing contact with the sexy Army Ranger officer she'd met in college, right before he'd joined the FBI.

Well, maybe *comfortable* might be the wrong word, since it had been around six months since she'd last had contact with him and over two years since she'd last seen him. She wasn't even sure if the e-mail address she had for him would even work anymore. And due to a certain…tension between them when they'd last been in contact, he might not want to see her in person now.

But even if he passed her off to someone else once he heard her out, she knew without a doubt that he'd help her. Her trust in him was still rock solid, even if the last e-mail she'd sent him had effectively cut contact. For a variety of reasons, most importantly her sanity.

But this was too important. If she was right about Tim, she and her brother might be in some kind of danger.

Mind made up, she scrolled through her phone's contact list, found Jake Evers's information and fired off an urgent e-mail.

****

"Did you get it?" his contact asked in their language.

Xang paused outside the restaurant to peer through the window and make sure his friends were still seated at the table before answering the man on the other end of the phone. The early April evening was warm, but a cool breeze blew in off the water, making him grateful for the dark hoodie he wore. And its pockets gave him ample room to hide what he'd stolen.

"Yes. Two USB drives, and I think one contains information about the target you're interested in. I didn't have time to go through everything but I'm sure this has what you're looking for." He was incredibly relieved about that, since the deadline had been coming up fast. He didn't dare fail his first unsupervised mission with the cell. This was finally his chance to prove his worth as something more than just a hacker, something they could find easily enough and replace him.

The cell leaders' endgame was vastly different from his. They wanted to inflict mass casualties on American soil, cause enough panic and chaos to shine a spotlight on the plight of their people. More than that, they wanted these attacks to damage relations between China and the U.S, and ultimately one day, force the Chinese government to grant his people an independent state.

For Xang, this jihad was far more personal.

It had taken him over three years to reach this point, where he was finally in a position to avenge his brother's and father's deaths at the hands of the communist

Chinese government. Murders, he corrected himself, fingers tightening around the phone. As strong as they were, they no doubt would have begged for mercy for an end to their suffering. And found none.

Xang would be just as merciless with the enemy.

"Excellent," the man said. "When can you get them to me?"

"Either later tonight or tomorrow morning."

His contact grunted. "What about the woman?"

"I'm with her brother right now. We were at her place earlier, but we left after they got into a fight. I think it was about me."

"She suspects you?" he asked in a hard tone.

"That I took the drives, yes, but I don't think she knows anything else." He'd intended to copy the files onto his own thumb drive but Rachel had come home before he'd had the chance and his only option had been to take them. He hadn't realized she'd noticed them missing until Brandon told him. He might have been worried she'd call the cops but she didn't have his cell number and had no idea where he lived. She didn't even know his real name.

"How can you be sure?"

Xang pondered that a moment. Though he'd only met Rachel a handful of times, he knew she didn't like or trust him. She was a lot more insightful than her little brother when it came to people's characters. "She doesn't know anything about me, and neither does the brother. It's fine." They had no idea who he was.

"What about the brother, does he think you did it?"

"I told him I didn't, and he seemed to believe me." Despite the close bond Brandon and Rachel shared, there was definitely some sibling rivalry going on in the family dynamics that they could potentially capitalize on later, if need be. "She acts more like a mother to him than an older sister. He hates it. We can use that if we need to."

"Good. I'll expect you by noon tomorrow with the drives."

"I'll be there." To get his first cash payment for the job, and to go over how the leader wanted to handle the next part of this op.

He slid his phone back into his pocket and re-entered the restaurant. His new American "friends" looked up at him as he approached the table, and Brandon smiled and scooted over to make room for him in the booth.

Xang took the seat and pretended to engage in the meaningless conversation going on around him, even smiled when required to, the whole time anticipating getting his hands on that cash tomorrow, and hopefully receiving even more brutal orders to execute as the deadline approached.

The four other men around the table continued talking and laughing, oblivious to what was taking shape around them. He loathed them all for their ignorance, for their patriotic love for a corrupt country and a regime that supported such a huge trade relationship with China and the godless government that had brutally suppressed his people and their rights for generations.

They had no clue what was coming here to the city, that the coming attack would take place at a joint Chinese and American target. Both countries were anti-Islamic that had shed innocent Muslim blood while the rest of the world looked on without doing anything. Both were populated by infidels and deserved to be destroyed. Xang was merely one of Allah's warriors bringing the fight to the American capital.

He loved the rush of having all that secret knowledge to himself. Savored knowing the irony that these men considered him a friend, or that they thought they were being kind by allowing him to hang out with them when in reality he was using them.

Xang hid a smile as the waitress brought their food. He was Chinese by birth, no more than that, and Muslim by Allah's grace because of his true people's blood. Finally being able to take part in an operation to wage jihad on U.S. soil was a total rush, more addictive than anything he'd ever been involved in before. The best part about this was the Americans' ignorance about his cell's existence—his *people's* very existence for that matter, let alone their plight. But the U.S. would suffer for that neglect very soon.

He hid a sneer as Brandon took a bite of his BLT, disgusted by the American and Chinese practice of eating pork. It was unclean and revolting and a sin against Allah.

And Allah always punished those who sinned against Him and the true believers.

Taking a sip of his soda, he pretended to laugh along with the others at some joke Ray made, all the while secretly reveling in their cluelessness. His time was near.

Vengeance, religion and politics aside, Xang planned to come out of this with enough money and contacts to start his own, deadlier cell, then wage jihad on his terms on both American and Chinese soil. He'd use whatever means available to him to attain that dream and avenge his father and brother—including everyone at this table—and not lose a moment's sleep over it.

Chapter Two

Jake thanked the waitress as he held out his coffee cup for a warm-up and flicked another glance toward the café's front door. He'd arrived early, twenty minutes ago now, and knew Rachel would be walking in any minute. The woman had always been a stickler for being on time, so even if it had been two years since he'd last seen her and half a year since they'd last had contact he was sure she wouldn't have changed that much.

Her message had sure come as one hell of a shock.

It still stunned him that she'd contacted him after all this time. After another week spent training in his team's relentless schedule he'd been looking forward to a weekend of downtime with the guys, and the last thing he'd expected when he'd checked his e-mails first thing this morning was to find one from Rachel.

I don't know if this will reach you or if you're even stateside right now, but I need to talk to you about something urgent. In person, if possible, but over the phone if you're not in the area anymore. I'm still in Baltimore. Please let me know ASAP. Rachel.

She'd sent it at just after oh-one-hundred-hours this morning, and that set his instincts jangling all on its own, but he'd also picked up on her palpable concern in the message.

He'd been surprised enough to see her name in his inbox, let alone that she'd reached out to him about whatever had happened, since she was the one to make it clear six months ago that she didn't want further contact with him. There was only one reason he could think of to warrant such a message after all this time: she was in trouble. Just the thought of it brought all his protective instincts roaring to the surface.

He hadn't seen her for over two years. He was thirty-two now and she'd be twenty-seven. They'd met back in college when she'd started tutoring him in physics and they'd quickly become good friends—and could have been so much more if he hadn't let them drift apart—so making the hour long drive to Silver Spring from Quantico was nothing. If Rachel needed him, he'd be there.

A flash of movement at the door caught his attention. He caught sight of a woman's shapely silhouette through the frosted glass, and when it swung open to reveal Rachel standing there, he felt like an invisible fist had reached into his chest and squeezed the air out of his lungs. She scanned the café, head high, posture erect, and when those hazel-green eyes landed on him he felt a ripple of primal awareness punch through him. Jesus, all this time later and the sight of her still took his breath away.

An expression of relief flashed across her pretty face when she saw him but then she seemed to falter for a second before offering a hesitant smile that made his hand tighten around his coffee cup. He hated that seeing him again made her uneasy, but he knew it was his own fault. God knew he regretted not going after her. Back then he'd had his reasons for letting her go. At the time they'd seemed like good reasons, too. Staring at her now, starved for the sight of her, it merely confirmed what he'd known all along.

He'd been a fucking idiot.

While on assignment with the NSA team, hunting for Hassani in Afghanistan and Pakistan, the shit he'd seen had made him realize what a huge mistake he'd made in letting her go. He'd finally been able to contact her after coming back stateside, only to receive a polite but firm response basically telling him that she'd moved on and not to contact her anymore. Which was why he was eternally grateful for that e-mail this morning.

Relaxing his grip on his mug, he nodded at her once. He stood to wait for her, never taking his eyes off her as she crossed to his booth. Her biracial features were a fascinating blend of Scots-Irish father, and Asian, given to her by her American father and Chinese mother respectively. She was dressed casually in a pale pink top that hugged her slender frame and emphasized the pert curve of her breasts in a damn distracting way.

The snug, dark denim skirt hit her several inches above the knee, giving him an eyeful of the toned muscles in those killer legs, set off by the wedge heels she had on. She wore her dark brown hair loose around her shoulders in shiny waves he'd always wanted to run his fingers through. Not that he'd ever get the chance now.

"Hi," she said as she reached the table, the smile slipping a little as she stopped on the opposite side of the booth as though unsure how close she should get.

"Hey. Been a long time," he said. *Way too long.*

"Yes." Delicate color stole into her smooth, golden-toned face as she seemed to hesitate again, like she wasn't sure whether she should shake his hand or just sit.

Screw that.

Hating the awkwardness between them, wanting an

23

end to it, Jake reached out and drew her into his arms for a quick hug, trying but failing to ignore how the feel and smell of her affected him. "How've you been?"

She returned the embrace and seemed to relax a bit, but the imprint of her lithe body against his and her sweet vanilla scent reminded him of all the reasons why he'd kept his distance from her in the first place. Shit, she felt good. Even better than he remembered.

"Good. You?" She pulled back far enough to put some distance between them and look into his eyes.

"Good," he echoed, and gestured for her to sit. When she'd settled into the booth he sat down across from her. "It was a nice surprise to hear from you."

That faint blush in her cheeks deepened. "I'm glad. I wasn't even sure if that e-mail address would work anymore."

His personal one that he only gave out to a select handful of people. But that wouldn't mean anything to her at this point. They were virtual strangers now.

Letting his famished gaze catalogue her features once more, he got to the point. "So. You okay? Your message sounded like something bad had happened."

"Yeah, I just have some information I wanted to report. I'm not a hundred percent positive that I'm right so I wanted someone I could trust in case I'm wrong, and you were the first person who came to mind."

Though he liked knowing she still trusted him that much, he frowned in concern. "What's going on? Are you in some kind of trouble?" Whatever it was, he'd make sure he handled it.

"I'm not sure," she admitted, lowering her gaze to her lap. "If I'm wrong about everything at least with you I won't feel like a total idiot, and if I'm right, then…" She shrugged and glanced around as if to make sure no one was listening in, and his protective instincts began to hum louder. Rachel was the least flighty and drama-prone woman he knew, so if she thought something was wrong then it likely was and he wanted to know exactly what they were dealing with.

He lowered his voice as he leaned forward more. "What's going on?"

Rachel sighed. "It's someone my brother's been hanging around with lately, over the last month or so, I guess. I think I saw him on the FBI's Most Wanted list last night, right before I e-mailed you."

His eyebrows shot up in astonishment. Why the hell was Brandon hanging out with someone on the Most Wanted list? "Who is he?"

She dug her phone out of her purse and accessed the list. "I think this is him," she said quietly, holding the screen toward him.

Jake studied the picture for a moment before reading the name below it. Xang Xu. Not familiar to him, but the guy was listed for international cyber crimes. Wasn't Jake's department, but he could put her in touch with the right people and in the meantime he sure as hell would take measures to ensure she and her brother were safe.

He looked up at her. "How sure are you, and why?"

"I'm ninety-five percent sure it's him, because he's been over to my place a few times. Except my brother knows him as Tim. And he worries me."

Concern buzzing in his gut, Jake set his forearms on the table and leaned toward her. "In what way?"

"He's creepy. Shifty. And he's shown a really bizarre interest in me—well, not me personally so much," she rushed to add when Jake's expression darkened, "but my work. From the first time I met him he asked me really detailed questions about my job, the firm, what I do there and what projects I'm involved in. I gave him the bare minimum to be polite and brushed off the rest of the questions, but he wouldn't let it go. It's almost like he hangs out with my brother just to be able to see me, which is really weird."

He did not like where this was going. Not at all. It was all too easy for him to picture this Xang guy developing a sexual fixation on someone as gorgeous and accomplished as Rachel. The primal male in him wanted to hunt the asshole down and pound the shit out of him as a warning to stay the hell away from her.

"Has he ever made a move on you or anything? Left you messages of some sort? Followed you?"

"No, nothing like that. It's so bizarre. And then yesterday I found out my brother gave him access to files on my personal laptop at home. Brandon and I got into an argument about it. Then I noticed a USB drive was missing and when I assumed Tim had taken it, Brandon stormed out with Tim and the others. Later I found another drive missing as well. And the other, more worrisome thing is the stuff I've overheard Tim talking about. Radical, anti-government stuff. About how the country deserves to 'burn in the hell it's created'," she said, using her fingers as air quote marks. "I was already suspicious that something bad might be happening, and then I saw his picture on TV."

Yeah, none of this sounded good. "You warn your brother about this?"

"He won't answer my calls so I left a few texts for him but he hasn't responded to them. Even if he does, I don't think he'll listen until I have hard evidence to back everything up."

"Like Tim stealing the USB drives and seeing him on the list isn't evidence enough?"

She shook her head. "He didn't want to believe the theft part when it happened, because he knows I don't like the guy in the first place. And until I know for sure the guy in the picture is Tim, he's not going to listen."

Yeah, and that only meant she was a good judge of

character, as far as he was concerned. "What would the guy want with your work files, anyway?" As far as he knew she designed high-end homes and other buildings, not banks, casinos or military installations that might be an appealing target for a hacker like Xang.

"I don't know, but I'm betting it's not because of a deep, burning curiosity about architecture." She stopped when the waitress approached to offer coffee, and handed her a menu. Rachel glanced at him questioningly.

He gave her a small smile to put her at ease. "Go ahead and order something. We'll talk more afterward."

They ordered and the waitress left. "So," Rachel said, wrapping her hands around her coffee cup.

He noted the lack of a ring on her left hand, and damned if he didn't feel a long-buried spurt of hope that it might not be too late for them. Which was fucked-up. He'd had his chance to claim her and hadn't. She'd moved on, was probably with Mr. Right now. "You think I'm onto something?"

"Sounds like. Let me make a call." He pulled out his phone and dialed one of his contacts at the Baltimore field office, told him he had possible info on someone on the Most Wanted list, and that he could expect them to come in within the next two hours.

Hanging up, he looked at Rachel. "After we eat I'll take you in to the local field office and we'll see what they have to say. They'll pull everything in the meantime and be ready for us."

"Okay. Thanks." She seemed relieved by the "us" part, or maybe that he'd be staying with her. Had she assumed he'd just walk away after this?

Not a chance. "No problem." He leaned back against the vinyl booth. "So you're still working at that big architectural firm, huh?"

"Yes. They get some good contracts," she said with

a shrug.

"Now you're just being modest."

She smiled impishly and didn't deny it, and he was reminded of why he'd always liked her so much. Rachel was brilliant and talented without any of the ego that someone with her résumé could easily have.

Taking him totally off guard, she reached across the table and drew her fingers down the side of his bearded cheek. "What's with this?"

Even through the thick growth of whiskers he felt her touch like an electrical shock across his cheek. Jesus, what the hell would it be like if she ran her fingers over his naked body? His heart rate kicked up at the thought and he shifted slightly against the seat.

For a second he struggled to form an answer. "I've uh, been working overseas. On a job with another security team." Titanium Security, to be exact.

Her smile widened. "It looks good on you. Very badass."

He laughed at the compliment, pleased that she liked what she saw. "Thanks."

"And what do you mean, with another security team? Did the people at you-know-where not come to their senses and give you your dream job yet?"

He appreciated her faith in him and that she was being careful with her wording here in public. He didn't like people knowing he was a federal agent, and he hated the inevitable questions it always brought. But Rachel had known that making the HRT was his dream ever since leaving the Army to join the FBI, which he'd done right after graduating from college.

"Technically I was on loan for the job," he explained. "My full-time job's pretty great, though. Demanding, but I love it."

Rachel blinked, then frowned and lowered her voice. "So...you made it?"

He merely smiled and took a sip of coffee, neither confirming nor denying it.

"Oh my God, you did!" She beamed at him, the warmth of her smile hitting him right in the sternum. Damn, he'd missed her, more than he'd even realized until she'd walked through that door a few minutes ago. "I'm so happy for you. Not that I had any doubt you'd make it someday, because they'd be stupid not to have you."

Her absolute faith in him and his abilities touched him. And because he couldn't discuss it in public and didn't know how to respond, he changed the subject. "You look good."

Her gaze snapped to his, and he saw a flash of feminine awareness there before she masked it. "Thanks. You do, too." She let her eyes travel over his upper body, and if he wasn't mistaken there was an appreciative gleam in her eyes. "You're bigger than you used to be."

"Yeah, a bit." He'd put on a solid fifteen pounds of muscle since joining the HRT, due to the relentless PT and training. He ran a hand over his chest, pleased when her gaze tracked the movement. He couldn't help it if he got off on knowing she liked what she saw, and that she seemed to still be attracted to him.

Clearing her throat, she darted a quick glance down at his left hand, wrapped around his cup—checking for a wedding band?—then up to his face. "Are you and Linda still—"

He shook his head once, the movement emphatic. "We never got back together after you last saw us at dinner that night."

She blinked in surprise. "Oh. I'm sorry."

"Don't be. It was for the best."

"Oh," she said again. He couldn't be sure, but he thought he detected a hint of confusion in those pretty hazel eyes. "May I ask why?" she said softly. There was a slight note of accusation to her words, maybe even hurt as to why he hadn't told her. He wasn't ready for that conversation yet, but he could answer the question she'd asked.

Because she wasn't you. He didn't have the balls to tell her that much though. Not yet, anyway.

"Mostly we just weren't compatible. Once I started with the agency, my training and travel schedule got even more intense. Minimum term of my current job is four years, so if she wasn't willing to live with my schedule the way it was back then, then she sure wasn't going to be happy with what I do now, so..." He trailed off, letting Rachel figure out the rest of it herself while sparing her the details about the slow death of the relationship.

Looking back, he couldn't believe they'd both stayed in it for as long as they had. When he thought of all the fights about him not being there enough, the lengthy silences and absences, Linda's frequent teary outbursts and the cold shoulder when he returned from a training trip or course, it seemed so stupid. "The split wasn't bitter or anything. In the end we both recognized that we should have ended things way sooner. She's engaged now, to a cop in New Orleans." But enough about that. "What about you?"

She shook her head. "No, no one since about five months ago. We weren't a good match, as it turns out, much like Landon and I weren't."

The guy she'd been dating back in college. Jake withheld the comment that he could have told her on day one that Landon hadn't been good enough for her.

He didn't think any guy was though, least of all him, but if he ever got the chance, God knew he'd treat her right. Rachel was the sort of woman you cherished. And he definitely would.

As a poignant silence spread between them while they stared at each other, Jake knew they were thinking the same thing: that they were both single and available. Finally. After all this time.

Except now they hardly knew each other anymore and the demanding tempo of his job meant any woman in his life would have to come a distant second to his work schedule. Rachel wouldn't be any happier in that situation than Linda had been, and with him gone so much it wasn't fair for Jake to ask her for that kind of sacrifice right out of the gate.

But that didn't mean the attraction and the feelings weren't still there. Time and distance hadn't done a damn thing to diminish those. They were every bit as strong as they had been, at least on his part.

Rachel sat back with an almost relieved expression when the waitress appeared with their breakfasts. They steered clear of discussing their relationship statuses throughout the meal. While they ate they made small talk about mutual friends from their college days, when he'd been there using his GI Bill.

He couldn't help but let his attention wander to her hands and mouth. She had graceful, delicate hands with slim fingers. He'd always thought they were one of her most beautiful features, along with her pretty hazel-green eyes.

As she forked up a bite of crepe his gaze transferred from the elegant French manicured nails to her mouth and he stared at those full, pink lips while she chewed. Since meeting her he'd had countless fantasies about those hands and mouth, about what they'd feel like on his skin as they roamed all over his naked body.

He'd also had plenty of fantasies about the things he'd do to her if he ever got her naked beneath him. He wanted to find out what she felt like, the sounds she'd make while he explored her naked body with his hands and mouth.

It had started back when he'd still been with Linda, near the end, and they'd never gone away. Fantasizing about Rachel while he'd been in another relationship wasn't something he was proud of, but at least he hadn't acted on his growing feelings for her back then. He wasn't that much of an asshole.

Rachel glanced up from across the table, caught him staring, and that was enough to kick his brain back out of the gutter.

He stole covert glances at her throughout the rest of the meal, enjoying just being near her again. Rachel had an innate, graceful sensuality he wasn't sure she was even aware of, and it was so damn sexy he had to force himself to hold his answering desire in check and stop from reaching out just to touch the curve of her cheek. The urge to touch her, lay some kind of claim to her right here in front of everyone was damn near overwhelming.

When the waitress came back to gather their plates he snagged the bill before Rachel could and paid it over her protests. "You can get it next time," he said, glad when she didn't argue or say there wouldn't be a next time. Now that she'd reappeared in his life, he didn't ever want to lose her again.

Bullshit. You know you can't just be her friend. You never could.

It was true. He'd been very aware of that as the weeks of their final semester passed and his feelings for her intensified. So had Linda.

Pushing a pang of regret away, he stood and grabbed his jacket. "Ready?"

"Yes." She followed him to the door. "Should I follow you, or…"

"I'll drive. It's not far. Come on." He led her out to his truck and opened the door for her. It was a long way up into the cab, and when she went to put her foot on the running board, he took her arm and helped boost her up into the front passenger seat.

She flashed him an almost shy smile at the contact and tucked a shiny lock of hair behind her ear. "Thanks. And thanks for breakfast."

"You're welcome." He shut the door, rounded the hood and slid behind the wheel. It felt surreal to have her sitting next to him after so long. He had few regrets, but at that moment he wished he could go back and fix his mistakes—break it off with Linda early on instead of stubbornly trying to stick it out, and admit the full extent of his feelings for Rachel. Not that he hadn't had his chance right after they'd broken up.

Even after he was single he'd held off on going after Rachel because he wanted to be fair to her and he'd recognized that he wasn't ready to be in another committed relationship so soon after coming off a failed long-term relationship with Linda. Part of him had realized that what he felt for Rachel was even more intense and he'd known he wasn't in the right headspace to give her what she deserved. And in the time he'd taken to find his center again and fully realize what she meant to him, she'd moved on.

He'd told himself six months ago that there had to be a reason. That it was for the best.

What a bunch of bullshit.

He'd promised himself more than two years ago that if he ever crossed the line from friends to lovers with Rachel it wouldn't be for a fling. Simple fact was, with her it was all or nothing and back then he'd known he couldn't give her all of him.

But he could now, if she was willing to accept that his work had to come first. That was non-negotiable, and a sacrifice he'd been prepared to make when he'd tried out for the team. Would she accept that? Accept him after all this time?

That distracting thought kept looping through his brain as they talked on the drive over to the field office. It didn't take long. A little disappointing, since he wanted more time alone with her, but if he had his way he wouldn't be taking her back to her car until after a leisurely dinner at a romantic restaurant.

Inside, his contact met them at reception and took them back into a private office at the rear of the building. Rachel repeated the information she had on Xang. She didn't seem nervous while she gave her statement, but Jake could see how fast her pulse was beating in her throat and he made sure to stand in her line of vision in a silent show of support. Her poise was something he admired as much as her gentle heart.

When she mentioned the anti-government language "Tim" had used and picked out his photo on the Most Wanted list, the agent's brows lowered in apparent alarm. Jake straightened, watching the man's reaction closely as he picked up the landline and made a call. Within minutes three more agents were in the room, gathered around the desk as she repeated the story.

At the look they exchanged as she fell silent, she shot him a nervous glance and Jake stepped nearer, close enough to her side that he could feel her body heat and smell her clean, sweet scent.

"What?" she asked them finally when nobody told her what was going on.

The agent Jake had called initially, Travers, dropped into the chair behind the desk and leaned back, holding her gaze, his pale blue eyes intent on her face. "Any markings or tattoos you can recall on him?"

Her brow furrowed as she thought about it. "There's a tattoo of the Mandarin character for justice on his left shoulder. And on the inside of his...right forearm there's a kind of crescent moon, I think."

Travers, a senior agent with the domestic terrorist division in his mid-forties, looked at the other two men and Jake folded his arms. They knew something important. "What's up?"

The agent shifted his gaze to him. "That's Xang, without a doubt. And you say he's been going to the University of Maryland, College Park?"

She nodded. "For the past few months or so, yes. Why?"

When Travers didn't answer right away, Jake spoke up, his instincts on alert. "She's with me," he announced, setting a protective arm around her shoulders—and yeah, he knew it was a possessive gesture, he just didn't care what the other agents thought about it. "I've known her a long time, so unless you need her to leave the room because of security clearance issues, say it."

"He's been linked to an Islamic terror cell backed in Western China. In Xinjiang," one of the other agents said flatly.

Rachel sucked in a sharp breath, drawing Jake's gaze to her. At the shock on her face, he tightened his arm, registering the tension in her slender frame. It was obvious she knew of the region and the terror attacks that had happened there recently. "Rachel?"

She was staring at the other agent. "Is he a Uyghur?"

Jake's attention sharpened when the agent nodded, confirming that Xang belonged to the ethnic group descended from Turkic origins and now living in eastern and central Asia. The majority of who were Muslims.

"Partly, anyway," the agent continued. "He's got some family members in Xinjiang. Spent a few years in his teens living there with an uncle who was known to frequent a radical madrasa, before Xang moved back to Beijing at the insistence of his grandfather."

"But what about his tattoos?" she asked. "I thought that's against Islam. Isn't it considered desecrating the body?"

"Yes, but Xang's not your average Islamist. He's half Uyghur and half Chinese, and he uses that to his advantage so he can mesh with either culture."

Jake looked more closely at the Most Wanted list photo. Now that he was paying closer attention, Xang's features definitely weren't classical Chinese; they had more of a Eurasian look to them. And the crescent moon tat Rachel had noticed made all kinds of sense now, since it was the symbol of a terror group Jake had been briefed about a few weeks ago when he'd been working with Alex Rycroft's handpicked NSA team and the Titanium Security crew.

He looked back at Travers, trying to put the pieces together but nothing made sense. Why befriend Rachel's brother just to steal building plans? If this asshole had targeted Rachel for whatever reason, if she was in danger, Jake needed to know. Now. "So what the hell was he doing stealing documents from Rachel's place yesterday?"

Rather than answer, Travers turned his pale gaze on her. "Exactly what was on those USB drives?"

"I can give you a list of what I remember. For the rest, we'll need to access my server at work."

Travers stood. "And we're gonna need to talk to your brother and find out what else Xang has been up to."

Chapter Three

Rachel accessed the main server in her office at Edge Architectural Firm and searched through the stored files while Jake and two other FBI agents stood by. Because of the kinds of contracts the company took on, the server had all kinds of layers of protection on it so she couldn't access it remotely.

She'd already spent the past couple hours compiling a list of the things she remembered being on both stolen USB drives, but she was worried that she might have forgotten something important. Since they didn't know what Xang wanted with the files, they had to examine everything that might be in them in case it gave investigators important clues. She suspected they already had several theories but so far no one was telling her anything. And everything she came up with made her blood run cold.

"Here," she said to Agent Travers, pushing her chair back to let him have a better look at the computer screen. "This is the list of potential files I copied over the past few months."

She stood and gave him her chair, rounding the desk to join Jake. He stood leaning against the wall as he watched the proceedings, thick arms folded across his chest, his jeans and black T-shirt hugging his muscular frame. His deep brown hair was cut short but that heavy scruff on the lower half of his face made him look a bit dangerous. Six-foot-one of tall, dark and handsome right there in front of her. In any other circumstance he would have proved a huge distraction. Right now all she cared about was helping the agents find her brother and help them get a break in the case.

"Your brother respond to your texts yet?" Jake asked as she came to stand beside him.

Someone back at the field office was tracking Brandon's cell phone to try and find him. "No, but my bosses did. They're coming in the next hour to talk to them." She nodded at the agents surrounding her computer.

He nodded. "Good. In the meantime, keep trying your brother." He turned to the others. "You guys good here for a while so I can take her home for a bit? I'll need a crime scene team and one of your tech people."

"Yeah, we've got the warrant, so go ahead," Travers answered, not bothering to look up from the monitor as he ordered a male agent named Kim to go with them and told someone else to send the crime scene team over there.

Jake took her elbow to lead her out of the room and the feel of his strong but gentle fingers wrapped around her arm caused a shiver of sensation to cascade through her. He was even more built now than he had been back in college and the memory of how much his nearness affected her didn't come close to the reality. The strained awkwardness she'd feared from him when she walked into the diner hadn't lasted beyond that hug and now it was as if that long separation had never happened. They still clicked, the same as they always had.

Just being next to him like this made her feel delicate and feminine, protected and cherished. Knowing he was single made her imagine all over again what it would be like to be with him. But they'd only just reconnected and she wasn't even sure he'd be interested in her that way anymore. Besides, he was here to help her with the situation at hand and she knew him well enough to realize he wouldn't be anything but professional while he was here on official business.

Jake ushered her back down to his truck, helped her in, and drove her to her place while she gave directions. Pulling into the underground parking garage with the team following them, a stab of disappointment hit her when she didn't see Brandon's red compact in any of the visitor's parking spots.

"His car's not here," she murmured, wishing she could go back and do things differently yesterday. She might have unknowingly put him in danger by making him mad enough to storm out last night.

"He'll call you," Jake said, sounding totally confident even though he'd never actually met Brandon. He'd only ever heard about him and their complicated family dynamics from her. "The kid worships you, there's no way he's gonna ignore you for long, no matter how mad he is."

Being that she was the only relative he had on this side of the Pacific, that didn't console her much. Still, she knew Brandon loved her and continued to look up to her in a lot of ways, even if he'd never admit it. "Hope so. Well, come on up."

They stopped first to talk to security. Once Jake showed his FBI badge, things moved quickly and the guards accessed the surveillance camera footage from the previous day to see if they had any footage of Xang while the crime scene team headed up to her condo with Agent Kim. She and Jake followed a few minutes later.

After shutting the door behind them, she was overcome by a moment's unreality that Jake was actually standing inside her place. His size and the intensely masculine energy he radiated made the place feel so much smaller all of a sudden. All of her senses were hyperaware of him.

He looked around, taking everything in, and stopped when he caught her staring at him. "What?" he asked with a hint of a smile.

"I can't believe you're actually standing in my living room," she confessed.

For some reason the smile faded, replaced by an almost guarded expression. "Your laptop in one of the bedrooms?"

The abrupt transition in mood caught her off guard. Had she made him uncomfortable or something? "Wait, I meant that as a good thing. As in, I'm so glad you're here." She didn't know why he'd taken it differently, unless he was feeling more for her than he wanted to and had decided to close up.

The change in his expression was instant. His face softened and warmth returned to his dark eyes as he smiled. "Oh. That's good."

She grinned, shaking her head at him. "My laptop's in the guestroom, back this way." She led him down the tiled hallway to the guestroom. Kim was already at work on the laptop, still on the desk where she'd left it, so she guessed they must have already dusted for fingerprints. She could hear the crime scene team talking out on the balcony outside. "I looked through all the drawers yesterday and checked my room too, but nothing else is missing besides those two USB drives," she said to him and Jake.

Jake sat in the desk chair while Kim worked his magic on the keyboard. "Do you know if he copied anything off your hard drive as well?" Kim asked her without looking up from what he was doing.

"I'm not sure."

He grunted. "I'll be able to tell. Do you have a backup of the files that he might have been looking at?"

She verbally instructed him on where to find a couple of the designs in question—preliminary AutoCAD drawings for a new project she'd been assigned, a high-end luxury condo building on the outskirts of D.C. popular with the political elite. "This project isn't even close to being finished yet," she said, indicating the next one Kim pulled up. "The only reason I even brought these designs home is because I was going to work on it a little over the weekend."

Jake shifted behind her as Kim started going through the file. There were only a few notes, mostly just the bare outline and some measurements. He accessed her browser history next. "This look right to you?"

Putting a hand on the desk, she leaned forward to read the list of sites, trying not to be distracted by Jake's crisp, clean scent. God he smelled good. Focusing on the screen, she frowned. "Scroll down a bit."

Kim did, revealing more sites relating to architectural magazines and online articles. When he clicked on one it only took a moment for her to recognize a piece a local reporter had done on her at the grand opening of a local luxury hotel she'd helped work on.

"This was last year?" he said.

"Yes. Brandon said he'd been showing Tim some of my work, so I guess this was what he meant. What's the next one?"

Another article relating to a completed project she'd worked on two years ago. The next three links were all similar in content, all featuring something about her work on a particular building. She straightened, struck by the realization of how proud Brandon actually was of her if he'd been showing Tim all this. Even if he saw nothing wrong with Tim's weird obsession with her and her work. What was the connection between Tim and the plans though?

Jake and Kim exchanged a telling look. Then Jake straightened and looked at her, those espresso-brown eyes searching hers. "You sure he's never come onto you?"

She searched her memory, shook her head because while the way Tim—Xang, she corrected herself—stared at her was unnerving, he'd never tried to touch her or say or do anything sexually inappropriate. "I'm sure." Though the continued interest did seem like borderline stalker-type behavior.

Kim powered down then shut the laptop. "I'm gonna take this into the office and let the guys go through it. Prints already verified that Xang was on it yesterday, so now it's just a matter of figuring out exactly what he accessed and go from there."

"Sure." She'd feel better once they figured out what Xang wanted with the information he'd stolen.

"And where was the other USB drive?"

"In here." She pulled out the top left drawer of the desk and let him look through the contents. "There's nothing else missing. I wouldn't even have noticed the second drive if I hadn't been suspicious and started checking through my stuff."

"Well it's good you listened to your gut," Kim said. "This may be the break the agency needs to nail the guy." He stood and scooped the laptop off the desk.

Rachel eased to the side to let Agent Kim pass her and leave with her laptop. Her phone rang and she grabbed it from her pocket. When she saw the call display she exhaled in relief. "It's Brandon." Thank God. "Can I tell him about all this?"

Jake shook his head. "Not over the phone. Just make up something urgent and tell him you need him to come over right away."

Nodding, she turned away and answered. "Hey. You okay?"

"Yeah, fine. What's up?" His tone was cool but polite, letting her know he was still pissed about how she'd accused Tim.

"Where are you?"

"Out with some friends."

She bit her tongue to keep from asking if Tim was one of them, concerned only with getting her brother back here immediately. "Listen, I had an accident and my car's been towed. Can you come over?"

"Damn, are you all right?" He sounded genuinely worried, all lingering traces of anger gone.

"Just a bit sore, and shaken." Well, that last part was certainly true.

Brandon expelled a hard breath. "Damn, I'm glad you're okay. I'll come right now. Be over in twenty."

"Thanks," she said, aware that Jake was behind her, listening.

"Sure. You need anything?"

"Just to see you."

"Be there soon. If you change your mind about wanting something, let me know."

And there was the baby brother she knew and loved. Her throat thickened. Maybe having Jake here to back her up while she explained everything would make Brandon listen. "I will."

After ending the call she exhaled and faced Jake, once again taken off guard by the sight of him, all masculine power and dark good looks standing five feet away. He was staring at her, the naked male interest in his eyes setting off a burst of heat inside her.

Kind of pathetic that she'd never been able to let the idea of him go, but it was impossible to forget him and truly move on when she measured every other man against him. If he hadn't been leaving for a contract job overseas the morning after they'd said their goodbyes, she knew in her gut things would have turned out far differently for them. If he'd stayed, she would have gone to him and told him how she felt. Hell, she'd almost gone to the airport the next morning to do just that, then chickened out at the last moment because he'd still been with Linda.

Now she swallowed at the heated look in his eyes, her mind flashing back to that night etched so deeply into her memory.

Just the two of them, alone outside the restaurant with the full moon shining down on them. She wasn't even sure when things had begun to change, when their friendship had suddenly become more. But she'd never forget that goodbye.

Linda had gotten into an argument with him at the table and taken off in the middle of dinner, and looking back Rachel realized she must have picked up on the vibes between her and Jake. Rachel had stayed to finish dinner, trying to smooth things over and distract Jake from the fight, even as she'd been furious that Linda would do that to him the night before he shipped out for a contract job in Afghanistan. But the most telling part was that Jake hadn't gone after her or called her to make up before he left.

Instead, after dinner Jake had walked Rachel to her car. He'd stood close, staring down at her with an intensity she'd never seen from him before. Whether it was because he was fed up with Linda's drama or not, she'd allowed herself one insane moment of hope that he'd reach for her, tell her *she* was the one he wanted.

Then he'd curved a strong hand around the back of her neck and gazed deep into her eyes as he spoke.

I'd do anything for you. You know that, right?

She'd stood there and nodded, her throat too dry to

utter a single word in reply, even though the words were right there on her tongue. *Then end it with her and ask me to be yours.* It had taken everything she had to hold the reply back.

He didn't blink, didn't look away. His intent stare sent an almost electric current buzzing over her skin. For a few endless heartbeats she was convinced he was going to kiss her, but when she didn't respond he dropped his hand from her nape and pulled her into a tight hug instead.

Part of her had been disappointed in her cowardice, but in hindsight she knew she'd never be able to respect or trust him if he'd kissed her while in a relationship with someone else. Not that Linda was a bad person. Her relationship with Jake had already been strained at that point and, adding in the additional stressor of finding out her boyfriend had feelings for another woman... Yeah, Rachel could understand why she'd been so upset.

"He's coming over," she said to him now, a hot ball of need pooling in her abdomen as she pushed the memory away. Did he ever think about that night too, and wish things had gone differently?

The heat was still there in his eyes, but he'd banked it now. "Good. Was he with Xang?"

"Not sure, but it's possible. I didn't want to ask him in case it made things worse."

He nodded and tucked his phone away. "I want to head back down and talk to the security guys."

"Okay, I'll go with you." She headed out into the hall and toward the front door, pausing only long enough to grab her keys from the island.

When she looked over her shoulder Jake was staring at her again, the focus of that laser-like attention making her mind slip into vivid and erotic images of what it would be like to be the sole focus of that concentration in bed. She wasn't gutsy enough to call him on it or the attraction still simmering between them though. "What?"

"I like your place. It suits you."

She wasn't sure whether that was a compliment or not. "What do you mean?"

He shrugged. "Soothing. Elegant. Peaceful."

He thought she was all those things? "Thanks. I love it here. I bought it because of the view of the bay." Her fingers tightened around the keys. As much as she wanted to keep him here, keep him talking, she had to remind herself that he was only here to help and her brother could be in danger. But Jake had always made her feel so comfortable when she was with him. She'd missed his solid, unshakable presence in her life.

A wistful ache settled in her chest. "Remind me why we lost touch again?"

A flare of surprise registered in his eyes at the blunt question, but he didn't try to dodge it. "Dunno. But let's make sure it doesn't happen again."

She smiled, praying he meant there was a possibility of so much more between them than just as friends. "Deal. Now just let me grab a sweater." She turned to head to her room but one of the crime scene guys stood there, blocking her path. Though she didn't know him, the look on his face stopped her in her tracks.

"There's something you need to see back here," he said to her, flicking a glance at Jake.

Rachel followed him to her bedroom, her pulse thudding hard and fast in her throat. She felt Jake behind her as she paused in the doorway. When the agent stepped aside, she gasped. The contents of her lingerie drawer were dumped out all over the place. A rainbow of lace and silk covered her neatly made bed and the floor beside it like multi-color confetti.

A hand flew to her chest and she instinctively took a step back. Whoever had done this had been in here after she'd left this morning. And they'd somehow disabled her security system to do it. A wave of cold flashed through her. "Jake."

He must have heard the fear in her voice because his rapid treads sounded behind her and then he set a protective hand on her hip as he peered over her shoulder. "Shit."

Yeah, that pretty much summed it up.

She took another step back, recoiling from the sight before her and what it signified, stopping only when her back met the solid warmth of his chest. Swallowing, she scanned the room. Nothing appeared to be damaged. This was a deliberate, pointed message.

Jake eased her to the side and stepped past her into the room with the two other agents, surveying everything. His expression grew even blacker when he focused on something on the bed. He turned to her, his eyes burning with fury. "He sliced them."

He? "What?"

"Your underwear. He cut them up with something sharp."

Rachel swallowed hard to force the lump back down her throat, aware of the sudden increase in her pulse and breathing rate. It freaked her out that someone had managed to get past the security measures in the building, not to mention her privately installed alarm, and even more that they'd not only gone through her underwear but slashed them. From all the crime documentaries she'd watched, that spoke of sexual fixation and a deeply buried rage that obviously couldn't be contained anymore.

Her mind whirled, trying to make sense of it. The only possible suspect who came to mind was Xang, but that seemed crazy. He'd gotten what he wanted yesterday, hadn't he?

Jake crossed back to her, spun her around by the

47

shoulders. "Let's go. Don't touch anything. I'll call in a team while we talk to security downstairs."

In a fog she allowed him to propel her out the front door and down the elevator to the lobby, her legs shaky as hell. What would have happened if she'd been home alone when the break-in took place? It could have been her lying cut up on her bedroom floor rather than her panties. Her stomach rolled at the thought.

The security guard on duty at the front desk escorted them into the back room where the chief of security was waiting for them. "I'm Franconi. You Agent Evers?" the man asked.

"Yeah, and we've got a problem." After Jake explained everything the man's grim expression made Rachel pause. He didn't seem surprised by what had happened. It was as if he already knew someone had broken into her place.

Jake stepped up to the bank of screens in front of Franconi where he and another guard were reviewing footage from the security cameras. "What did you find?"

"Is this the guy you're looking for?" Franconi asked Rachel, indicating a segment of footage showing Brandon and his friends in the parking garage. She knew it was from the day before because she remembered Brandon wearing that blue plaid shirt.

"That's him there." She pointed to Xang, nearly a head shorter than her brother and the others.

Franconi grunted and allowed Jake to play the footage back several times. "I've made a copy of it for you," he said to Jake, then added, "There's more."

Jake cast Franconi a sharp look at the gruff tone, and the man tapped a button on the computer on the next screen over, bringing up a different camera angle. "This is from a camera mounted on the side of the building. It's well concealed, so only a trained expert would find it."

As Rachel watched, a male approached the camera. He wore a dark hoodie and kept his head bent so his face wasn't visible to the camera from that angle. He reached into his hoodie and withdrew something metallic.

"Leatherman tool," Jake muttered.

Whatever it was, the man brought it to the door handle and used it to jimmy the locking mechanism.

"He's smart enough to know how to pick the lock without triggering anything," Franconi said, "and it's possible he somehow disabled the camera mounted on the interior wall of the stairwell too, because it doesn't pick him up when he comes in."

Sure enough, seconds later the exterior door opened. "Why isn't the alarm going off?" Rachel asked.

"We don't know, but we think he must have disabled it ahead of time. Probably been casing the building for a few days at least. We're looking into it." On screen the intruder started to slip inside, pausing a moment to glance up and around. "This is the part I wanted you to see." He tapped a button on the keyboard in front of him, stopping the feed. When he moved back, she got her first good look at the man's profile.

Trepidation rippled through her. *Shit.*

She felt Jake stiffen next to her, then he moved in close, his gaze riveted to the screen. That's when she knew for certain it was Xang who'd picked the lock and snuck into the building. Fear raked her with its icy claws. "When was this?" Jake demanded.

Franconi glanced first at her, then Jake. "Just over two hours ago."

All the blood drained from Rachel's face as she was confronted with the certainty that her gut had been right about Xang all along. And also so very wrong. He could have raped her. Cut her.

"I was out. I'd gone to meet..." She trailed off, looking at Jake. "So he's been casing the building, waiting for me to leave so he can break into my place and do...that?"

"He took the stairs to the eighth floor, and the cameras pick him up exiting and walking in the direction of your place, but again, the cameras near your door weren't working. He comes into view again seven minutes after that back at the stairwell and leaves the building the same way he came in," the head of security finished, pulling up the footage.

Rachel watched it for a few minutes, then looked at Jake, her mind spinning. Had anything else been out of place and she'd missed it? She hadn't noticed anything else missing, but they hadn't checked anything except the desk.

"Xang broke into my place and cut up my underwear," she said in a voice that sounded strangely wooden with disbelief.

Jake stepped back and took her arm, snagging the USB drive containing the security footage with his other hand. "Come on." He spoke over his shoulder to the security agents on the way to the door. "I'll be in touch within the hour."

When he ushered her into the stairwell that led to the underground parking garage, she resisted. "Where are we going?"

"Taking you to the office to run these pictures of Xang through the facial recognition software to get an airtight ID on him. While that's happening the team will keep collecting evidence, and once they do the forensics we'll find out exactly what the hell we're dealing with. And until I know you're safe from that asshole, you're not coming back here."

She craned her head back to frown at him, feeling lost and freaked out of her mind. "Where am I supposed to go? For how long?" This was insane. She was angry and scared and outraged that Xang had victimized her this way. Her whole life had been upended in less than twenty-four hours.

"I'll let you know. Right now I need you to call your brother back and change the meeting place. We need to bring him in *now*."

As a shiver of foreboding snaked down her spine, Rachel got on the phone to Brandon. Thankfully he answered and she asked him to meet her at a restaurant close by, refusing to give him any details other than it was important he meet her there right away.

She hung up and followed Jake to his truck, her imagination conjuring up eyes watching their every move from the shadows. Xang wouldn't seriously be crazy enough to still be here, would he?

But when Jake kept glancing in his mirrors as if checking for someone following as he drove away from her building, she knew those fears weren't unfounded.

****

Xang pulled the hood of his hoodie off his head and replaced it with a ball cap as he walked away from the building at a fast clip and headed for the closest subway station with his heart pounding. That had been exhilarating in a way none of his stupid hack jobs had ever been.

His hands were trembling with excitement in his pockets, the right one rubbing over the treasure he'd taken with him. He'd waited just out of sight long enough to observe Rachel enter the underground parking in a newer model silver pickup driven by a man, then leave with him about a half hour later.

He was careful to keep his face averted during the journey so the CCTVs and security cameras on the subway didn't get a clear shot of him. Once back safely in the downtown Baltimore apartment he'd been loaned for the job, he used his burner phone to call his contact. The place was owned by someone in the network, a rich businessman back in mainland China. It was said he was connected to this current op and was tight with Xang's contact. He and the others were all watching Xang's progress closely. If he performed well, the potential for advancement within the organization and a lucrative payout were huge.

"I didn't find anything else," he told the man in their language when he answered, "but the woman showed up and left with a man I've never seen before. I texted some pictures to you."

Not the greatest quality since they'd been taken with his phone, but Xang hadn't been expecting anyone else to show up with her so it was all he'd had. He'd been lucky to get out of there undetected after his little redecorating project. Had they seen what he'd done in her place yet?

"You're sure no one saw you?"

They'd figure it out shortly, if they hadn't already, and Rachel would freak when she saw her room. He wished he could have seen her reaction, but that was way too risky, even for someone with his skills.

"I disabled a bunch of security cameras beforehand and silenced the alarm when I went in. I checked her place myself, every room, and didn't find anything more." Desperation had required him to take the significant risk of infiltrating Rachel's secure building. He didn't like having to do ops when he was desperate, but he'd had no choice this time.

"You need to get into her work server."

Xang pursed his lips. He was fucking well aware of what he *needed* to do, but it wasn't that simple. He had to figure out how to pull off this next dangerous step without getting caught.

It was already embarrassing enough that he, one of

the best hackers in the business, had so far been unable to crack the encryption on the server. It was an intranet, and from his initial research, much more sophisticated than pretty much anything he'd come across, with layers and layers of encryption that rivaled the damn NSA. Every time he'd tried to hack into the system so far had failed, much to his frustration.

It made him look like a fucking loser, when he was anything but. The only option now would be to break into her office building and try to access it from there. But he'd researched the firm and they hired the best security analysts in the world to keep everyone out, which was why he couldn't hack it from the outside.

That also meant that the odds of him walking away from the op without getting arrested or shot were way less than that of actually retrieving the damn files he needed.

"You need to do it tonight," his contact said. A command, no matter how quietly stated. Xang knew exactly what was happening.

They were testing him. It infuriated him. He'd already proven his loyalty and his skills—skills that included far more than being slick with a computer—more than once. If they hadn't given him such a tight timeline he might have been able to come up with a much better plan. This felt too much like he was flailing around in the dark, like they were setting him up to fail so he could take the fall.

"You brought me on board for this as a hacker," he reiterated, face burning with humiliation as the man forced him to point out the obvious—that he wasn't acting as a warrior this time. He was well aware that only his reputation and freedom were on the line if he got caught, and that they didn't give a shit about him other than his skill set and what he could do for them. Which was why he didn't plan to stay at the bottom rung of the cell's ladder after this op.

"Not my problem. I can't send in more resources without risking blowing the entire op. Get me those plans, tonight."

The threat was implicit in the man's tone. Xang knew exactly what sort of "resources" the man had out there, including a hit team he could send out on Xang with a single phone call.

He opened his mouth to argue but the man hung up before he could respond. Rage boiled inside him. Left alone in the room with his contact and the head of the cell, he could kill them both with nothing but a single knife—something he'd already proven to them when they'd checked into his past. They thought that just because they were rich that they could control him, render him less dangerous or less of a threat by making him act only as a hacker on this job. They didn't seem to understand that he had carried out their orders so far only because he *chose* to.

As he was about to put the phone down, Xang's personal cell buzzed with an incoming call. Brandon.

"Hey," he answered in Mandarin, playing it cool even though he was still pushing back the anger. He wasn't worried about security because he'd added plenty of encryption to the phone previously. "What's up?"

"Nothing. Hey, I know I asked you already, but are you sure you didn't take anything from my sister's place last night?"

"I told you I didn't." But he'd certainly left her a message today, he thought in satisfaction.

After the way she'd snubbed his attempts to win her over—like she was too good for him—and the inability to get the files he needed, scaring her had seemed like the perfect outlet for his frustration. She was just like everyone else, thinking she was better than him. Well, she wasn't, even if she was smart and fucking hot.

Posing as a college transfer student and hanging around Brandon for the past few weeks to get to her on direct order from the cell hadn't been that much of a hardship. When he'd checked her room this morning he'd come across her underwear, and they were every bit as sexy as she was. The idea had hit him then. Maybe they'd think he was after her and it would throw off any cops who started investigating him, at least long enough to allow him to do the rest of his job while they were distracted.

After he'd cut them up and scattered them across the bed and floor like those whacked-out stalkers did in movies, he'd stuffed one into his pocket on impulse for two reasons. To terrorize her, and to make her think this was about her personally, rather than the files he needed. With luck it would throw off any investigators long enough for him to skip town.

And besides, it gave him a rush to know he'd invaded her most personal domain and likely left a psychological mark on her. Made him understand why some guys got hooked on shit like that. Rape wasn't part of his credentials yet. Maybe he could change that with her.

"Why?" he demanded when Brandon didn't reply. Rubbing his fingers over the lacy thong in his pocket, imagining the look on Rachel's face when she saw what he'd done, he turned to face the tall windows that gave him a commanding view of the city and Chesapeake Bay in the distance.

The view was spectacular, the best money could buy, but what he enjoyed most was being able to look down on the world. From this height the people moving around on the sidewalks looked like insignificant little ants running around in their meaningless lives.

He'd lived like that once, back in Xinxiang with his family when he was young. Every day the same monotonous drudgery of struggling to find enough work to put food on the table. Then one day Chinese soldiers had come to take his father and older brother away, calling them terrorists for their affiliation with a radical group from their mosque.

Xang hadn't fully understood what had happened to them both after that; he'd only known that they never came back. It wasn't until he was older that some of the elders had shown him the pictures of what had been done to them that he'd truly understood and started on the path that had led him here.

Brandon sighed. "Look, man, just be straight with me. If you have something just give it back to me and I won't say anything."

"I don't have anything," he said, this time with a sharp edge to his tone.

A few seconds passed, as though Brandon was searching for the right words. "My sister just called to say she got into an accident earlier. I don't know how bad she's hurt, but she doesn't need to get in trouble at work because of missing files on top of that."

Xang was unmoved by the not-so-subtle plea for the USB drives, and if Brandon thought about it for two seconds he'd realize that even if Xang admitted it and returned them, he'd already have made himself copies.

Still, he frowned. Had she been in an accident? She *had* shown up in that guy's pickup. Or was the story a lie? It didn't sound like she'd told Brandon about the underwear thing. Why wouldn't she? Unless she hadn't noticed yet? She was quite intelligent. Xang had a feeling she was up to something.

His heart rate barely picked up at the thought. "Did she call the police?" Not that they'd find him. He might not be military or special-police trained but he knew enough about field craft to cover his tracks and make sure no one could trace him via phone or other electronic devices.

"She didn't say, but I assume so. Look, sorry, just forget I said anything, okay? I'll talk to you later."

"Yeah." He hung up and stared down at the busy city spread out below him, his for the taking once he got the money from this job and put it to good use buying pieces of Baltimore's underworld. Then he could continue the fight his father and brother had begun.

He was still admiring the view when the burner phone rang again a few minutes later. Xang answered immediately, already knowing who it was because his contact was the only one who knew the number. "What's up?"

"I thought you said no one saw you."

Xang's muscles tightened in reflex at the buried rage in that voice. For the first time a trickle of unease slid through him. "They didn't. Not other than some footage on the cameras I couldn't disable, and I kept my face pretty well concealed." He hadn't cared all that much about being seen on camera at the time, since he never planned to go back there.

"Well someone did, and the woman is on to you. I had someone run those pictures you sent through a Chinese security database. The man she was with has connections all over the military contracting world. Word is he's FBI now."

What? "That's impossible," he rasped, a sick feeling taking hold in his stomach. The security cameras would have picked him up from time to time as he moved through the building. Though he'd worn gloves, he'd no doubt left some DNA behind in her room, and with the underwear thing they'd be even more motivated to find him. *Shit.*

The man grunted in irritation. "Get out of there and disappear, but keep this line open and available. I've put my personal reputation on the line by recommending you for this op—you'd better do everything in your power not to ruin it."

Or else.

Xang heard the unspoken threat in those words and had no doubt it was real. One misstep and he was as good as dead, no matter how fancy he was with computers or how careful he was with his field craft. In the cell, there was always someone they could replace him with. His gaze shot to the full length windows, to the view he'd been admiring moments ago. There could be men down there hunting him right now, ready to take him out because of what he knew.

A ripple of trepidation shivered up his spine. He couldn't be taken or killed yet. Not now.

He moved back from the window, suddenly feeling paranoid. "I'm on it."

Xang hung up and ran a hand through his hair, frantically going over his options. No doubt about it—he was being hunted. He needed time to clear out of here and erase his tracks before either a hit team or law enforcement officials closed in on him.

At this point his only real chance of survival, let alone living long enough to collect his money at the end of this op and put his next plan into action, was to get himself some collateral. Lucky for him, he knew just where to find some.

But instead of going after it, he would bring the collateral to him.

Reassured by the feel of his weapon stuffed into the back of his waistband and the weight of the knife strapped to his calf beneath the leg of his jeans, he fished his personal cell out of his pocket once again and dialed Brandon, who answered on the first ring.

This plan would work. It had to. "Hey, I feel bad about your sister, especially now that I know she was in an accident." He paused, sighed for effect. "Are you on your way to her place?"

"No, she just called again and I'm meeting her somewhere else now, why?"

"Because…you're right. I took the files, and I'm sorry."

Brandon made a sound of outrage. "Tim, why the hell would you—"

He couldn't help the smile that spread across his face. This was almost too easy. "Meet me at the diner on the corner now and you can take them to her."

Chapter Four

O ut in the parking lot in his truck, Jake kept his eye on Rachel. She was seated at a window booth, waiting for her brother to show up at the restaurant they'd chosen, after she'd changed the meeting location. Having seen the state of her bedroom, there was no way in hell Jake was letting her stay in her building a second longer. The team was still going through her condo, but hadn't turned up anything new yet. Others had begun the hunt for Xang. With any luck, they'd have him in custody by nightfall.

For now, Jake needed peace of mind.

He dialed his roommate, Tuck, who picked up on the third ring with a drawled, "What's up, farmboy? You meet up with your mystery girl yet?"

Normally the dig at his Iowa roots amused him, but he was in anything but a happy mood at the moment. He knew Tuck and Bauer were curious about Rachel, since he'd dropped everything to rush out and meet her this morning. "Yeah, and I've got a bit of a situation."

Tuck hooted. "That was fast. Serves you right for ditching us for a chick. You're missin' out on some gorgeous conditions, by the way—we're just about to hit our first trail."

Jake had originally planned to go dirt biking with them, right up until the moment he'd seen that e-mail from Rachel. After that, there was no question where his priorities lay. "No, I mean as in this could be turning into a work situation."

A startled pause followed as Tuck digested that. "The hell did you do, man? You've only been gone a couple hours. Even you couldn't find trouble that quick." He sounded genuinely interested.

"Nothing," Jake said with tried patience. "Look, I don't want to go into details over the phone, but I need some backup. Unofficially," he added. Their overlapping work schedules should do fine for what he had in mind. And though Tuck loved to give him a hard time whenever possible—Jake was one of the newest members of the team, after all—he knew Jake would never ask him for a favor on their day off if it wasn't really important.

"Can you and Bauer meet me back at our place within the next couple hours?" He felt bad that it would end their dirt biking adventure before it had gotten started, because downtime was precious and Tuck sure as hell could use some R&R with everything that was going on in his personal life right now.

But Tuck didn't hesitate. "Whoa. Yeah, man, if you need us, we'll be there."

"Thanks."

"Don't worry about it, brother. We'll just add this to your tab."

"You do that," Jake replied with a grudging chuckle. The form of payment at the end of all this would no doubt be taken out in the form of food, alcohol, or some shitty-ass job no one else on the team wanted to do.

Hanging up, he already felt better knowing his buddies had his back in whatever was unfolding here.

Until he knew Rachel was no longer under threat, he wasn't taking any chances with her safety. It made his skin crawl to think of that asshole invading her place and pawing through her underwear.

Slashing a woman's underwear to pieces meant the guy had a shitload of rage underscored with sexual undertones and it was a definite warning sign that things could easily escalate to something like rape or worse. Jake wasn't going to let that happen, and the FBI team hunting Xang would be doubly motivated to bring him in before he did something worse.

A few minutes later there was still no sign of Brandon and Jake's phone buzzed with an incoming text from Rachel.

He's not here and won't respond to my messages.

They'd already been here nearly forty minutes. It should only have taken her brother fifteen to get there after their last conversation, and unless his phone had died in the past few minutes there was no reason for him not to reply to her. Jake didn't like the implications involved in all of this. *Come on out*, he texted back.

The diner door opened a few moments later and Rachel strode toward his truck, all poised, feminine grace with an aura of confidence that never failed to stir him. Letting her slip through his fingers had been a huge mistake, but he was a different person in a different place now and he wasn't making that same mistake again. The circumstances of their reunion sucked ass, but at least now he'd be spending a lot of time with her until this was dealt with. That was a start.

He hopped out to open the passenger door for her, taking in the tense set of her shoulders and the worried frown marring her brow. He wished he could make this go away for her.

"What now?" she asked, looking up at him as though she hoped he had the answer that would make everything all better. Unfortunately he had nothing.

"We'll wait a bit longer out here." He helped her up, shut the door and rounded the hood to climb back behind the wheel. Once inside the cab, he could practically feel the tension pulsing off her. "He might've been farther away than we thought when you last talked to him."

She shook her head, anxiously scanning the parking lot. "He said he'd be here in twenty. And he was really worried about me, so I know he'd come straight here." She turned those big, green-flecked eyes on him and he didn't even think—just reached out and curled his fingers around her hand. She gripped his tight in return. "Something's wrong."

Her skin was cold, her hand so delicate and fragile in his own. He rubbed his thumb across the back of her knuckles as he spoke. "We'll give him another fifteen minutes, and if he still doesn't show, we'll let the other agents know. Okay?"

She nodded and looked back out the window. "This isn't like him."

"We'll find him, no worries." His gut said otherwise. And dammit, he didn't want to be the one to have to tell her she was right about this. They sat in silence while they waited. He kept her hand tightly entwined with his while she checked the time on her phone every few minutes. When the hour mark came and went with no sign or contact from Brandon, he saw no point in keeping up pretenses. "Try him one more time."

She dialed, waited, and the call went straight to voicemail. Not bothering to leave another message, she ended the call and texted him again. He didn't respond.

Yeah, this was not good.

Jake fired the truck up and began driving as she typed out another text. Using his hands free device he called the other agents and explained that Brandon hadn't turned up, waited while they updated him.

"They've traced his phone to a metro station south of town about an hour ago. They're out looking for him now," he told Rachel after he hung up.

She set her phone down and clenched her hands in her lap, casting him a worried glance when he got on the highway and headed south from Baltimore. "Where are we going?"

"My place, near Quantico. I've called a couple buddies and asked them to meet us there, just as a precaution until we know what's going on. The field office will call when they know something more."

Her eyes were full of anxiety. "Do you think he's all right? Do you think Xang might have done something to him?"

"I'm sure he's fine," he said, but he was thinking exactly along the same lines as her.

She blew out a breath and closed her eyes. "I can't believe this is happening. God, I feel sick. I need to call my mom and let her know what's going on."

"Don't call her yet. No point in worrying her until we know more details."

"I just feel like I should be *doing* something."

"I know. But we've done all we can for now." Since he couldn't make this any easier for her and he respected her too much to give her pointless platitudes, he let a silence lapse between them. He could practically feel the tension humming inside her, and didn't know how to ease it.

"What about your family?" she finally asked him.

Her question surprised him, but he realized she was probably trying to distract herself. "They're all good. My parents are officially retired now and my brother and his wife have two little kids. They're all still back in Iowa. We get together for family holidays when my schedule allows. Christmas is a big deal but we don't usually get to celebrate it on the twenty-fifth."

She made a noise in her throat to show she was listening, that frown still in place. "My mom still flies here every year to spend Christmas with me, and now Brandon too."

"I'm glad. I bet you miss her."

"I miss her a lot, but she's still not ready to move back here. She's got her relatives there and she says being here reminds her too much of my dad, so…" She trailed off, her frown turning speculative. "These buddies of yours. Were you in the Rangers together?"

"No, but they're all former military." And he loved them all like brothers, same as he had the guys in his Ranger platoon. The time-intensive tempo of their schedules meant they spent a lot of time together— sometimes more than the guys did with their own families. The result was a tight, cohesive unit where every man trusted the others with his life. They sometimes fought and bitched at each other just like all brothers did, but at the end of the day, they had each others' backs.

She turned her head to study him. "So why are we going to see them?"

He didn't see the harm in telling her the truth, since she was going to find out anyway. "They're teammates of mine. I want to fill them in, have you get to know them a bit so you feel comfortable with them."

"Why?"

He shrugged, kept his eyes on the road. "I want them to help keep an eye on you. Our schedules rotate, depending on a lot of different things. I'm tied up with scheduled training most of the week if we don't get called out, so the guys can take over when I can't be there."

Her eyebrows shot upward. "You're putting a personal security detail on me?"

Wasn't exactly protocol to do it himself, but he and his teammates could protect her as well as anyone, and the control freak in him wanted to pick her detail himself. The guys he worked with were definitely the best. "Yes, ma'am. For now, anyway. If you're not comfortable with me and the guys doing it I can let the Baltimore office handle it, but you definitely need protection until this guy's brought in."

"What about my place and my job?"

There was no easy way to say it. "I think you know you can't go back to your place. And unless you can work remotely, you'll need to take some time off."

Rather than get pissed off or argue about it, she stared at him for a long moment before relenting with a sigh. "I'll talk to my bosses once I hear back about my brother."

"Sure, but given everything that's happened, they'll want you to take time away until this is all cleared up. And I wouldn't worry about them blaming you for the stolen files. You didn't do anything wrong."

It didn't surprise him that she was more worried about Brandon and her job than her own safety. Rachel was like that, always thinking of the people she cared about, putting them first. He'd once been included in that select group. He'd been stupid not to stay in touch more, a fucking moron to believe he could ever get over her.

All this time he'd told himself he'd been doing her a favor by letting their communications lapse, especially while he was overseas or in training at Quantico. She'd e-mailed him once a week without fail at first, never once chastising him if he didn't reply, but gradually they'd begun to trail off —whether she'd finally gotten fed up with him or she'd realized he wasn't worth her time, he wasn't sure—and he'd let them drift apart until she'd finally moved on.

Biggest mistake of his life. She wasn't Linda and it wasn't fair of him to assume she couldn't handle or want to adjust to the demands of his career.

When she didn't respond, only twisted her hands in her lap, he reached across the console to take her hand again. It was important to him that she understood she wasn't alone, that he wouldn't fade out of her life again. She had him to lean on now. "Whatever happens, I'm here for you, okay?"

At that she looked over and gave him a tremulous smile that made his chest ache as she squeezed his hand. "Thanks. I'm glad I called you."

"Me too." He was only sorry it had taken this for her to re-establish contact.

Wishing he could go back and undo all of that as he drove south toward Quantico, Jake vowed to make sure he never pushed her away again.

****

After an hour long drive, Jake finally turned the truck into a residential neighborhood and into the driveway of a two-story brick, traditional-style house.

"This is your place?" Rachel asked him as he parked beside another pickup with dirt bikes loaded into the bed, unable to hide her surprise.

"What, you expected a trailer park or something?" he said, his tone teasing.

"No, you just used to be a turnkey kind of guy. Condo or townhouse maybe. No yard, no maintenance, able to just lock the door and go whenever you want."

"Oh, that's still me. Just figured it was smarter to invest the money into a house rather than throw it out the window in rent each month. My buddy Tuck and I bought the place together. It's a good area. We should make a decent profit when we sell."

She nodded, hardly able to believe she was having this conversation when her brother had yet to respond and could potentially be missing. Her phone had remained silent in her lap the entire trip and Jake hadn't heard back yet from either the team at her place or the agents tracking Brandon's phone. It was maddening. She wanted answers, now, or she was going to go crazy. Feeling helpless sucked.

He led her through a neatly organized garage full of tools, sports gear and tactical gear, and into what she guessed was the mudroom. The smell of grilled meat hit her as soon as they stepped inside. With a solid hand planted at the small of her back, Jake ushered her through the mudroom to a spacious, newly renovated bright, country kitchen.

Two men were standing around the dark granite-topped island in the center of the room, one blond and the other huge with dark-hair, eating burgers. They both looked up when she and Jake entered.

"Guys, this is Rachel Granger," Jake told them.

The blond set down his burger and wiped his palm against his jeans as he strode over. "Hey, I'm Brad Tucker," he said in a warm Southern drawl. "You can call me Brad if you want, but most people call me Tuck." He stuck out the hand he'd just cleaned.

"Nice to meet you," she responded, gripping his big, callused hand. He looked older than Jake by a few years, and was several inches shorter but was just as broad through the chest and shoulders. His dirty-blond hair was cut into short waves that fell across his forehead and around his face, giving him a California surfer look. He had lively brown eyes that crinkled slightly at the corners as he smiled at her.

"And this is Clay Bauer," Jake added, nodding toward the giant of a man with the military short chocolate-brown hair.

He made no move to come around the island, so she stayed where she was, feeling like she was being scrutinized by those vivid blue eyes. He was the tallest of the three, and the most heavily muscled. One look at him and it was obvious he was a seasoned operator. Something about his set expression told her he wasn't too happy about her being there, as if he was suspicious of her and whatever trouble she'd brought to Jake's door, so she merely nodded in greeting and received the same in turn.

If Jake picked up on the chilly reception from his friend, he didn't let on. "You hungry? Thirsty?" he asked her.

The thought of eating at the moment made her feel nauseous. "Just some water would be great, thanks." Jake went to get it for her and she stood there awkwardly, not knowing what to say to fill the void as his friends watched her.

"So where do you know Jake from?" Tuck asked, back to munching on his burger.

"We took a few classes together in college and were in the same physics study group in our final semester." She left out the part about her tutoring him in case they teased him about it later.

Tuck stopped chewing and swung his head around to give Jake an astonished look. "Really? I never knew you could do physics, aside from windage calculations and stuff. Huh. Maybe we should start calling you Einstein instead of farmboy."

"Bite me, Tuck," Jake said from the refrigerator, where he was filling a glass with ice for her.

Grinning, Tuck faced her again. "He's so touchy sometimes. Like living with a moody teenager."

"I've never known Jake to be moody," she said, defending him automatically. She didn't know either man at the island at all, but it was way easier to imagine

Jake living with Tuck than Clay. She smiled her thanks to Jake when he returned with her water, ordering the nerves in her stomach to stop churning. She felt totally out of place here with his friends and she was worried as hell about Brandon.

"Why don't you go grab a seat out on the back deck while I fill these guys in on the details?" Jake said. It wasn't really a suggestion, only phrased as one, so she nodded and let herself out the sliding glass doors onto the wood deck.

Choosing a padded deck chair, she leaned back against the backrest and sighed as she surveyed the backyard. A tall privacy fence enclosed the tidy space, the lawn green and mowed short with military precision. There were no shrubs or flowers of any kind, just a stone patio below that housed an industrial-sized grill and a stone fire pit. Men loved their fire and grilling meat, and these guys were more alpha than most so it didn't surprise her. A few birds chirped from the branches of a large oak tree in one corner, the fresh green leaves rustling slightly in the breeze.

It should have soothed her but she was way beyond being soothed at the moment.

She mentally cringed as she thought of Jake inside, telling his teammates about Xang and Brandon. She wasn't sure if Jake had ever mentioned her to them in the past, but if he hadn't, this wasn't the kind of first impression she wanted to make. No matter what happened, she would absolutely not play the victim. She was stronger than that and would do whatever was necessary to help get her brother back and nail Xang.

She drummed her fingers on the arms of the wooden chair as she waited. The team at her place must have gone through everything by now, and the agents tracing Brandon's phone must know *something*. She hated being kept in the dark about everything, wished they'd at least give Jake updates so he could pass them on to her.

Her mother was going to freak when she learned about all this, and her bosses wouldn't be thrilled about the stolen plans or losing her until the investigators cleared her to go back to work. All that was out of her control though, and didn't matter next to Brandon's safety anyhow.

The sliding glass door opened a few minutes later and Jake stood there, giving her an encouraging grin. "Wanna come back in now?"

Preferring to talk about things inside and away from any potential eavesdroppers who might be in the neighboring yards, she carried her untouched water glass inside. Tuck and Clay were both still by the island but they'd finished eating, and judging from the hard expressions they wore and the way they had their arms folded across their chests, they hadn't liked what Jake had told them. Which meant they likely thought something bad had happened to her brother as well.

Rachel swallowed and followed Jake to the table where he pulled out a chair for her. With a murmur of thanks she sat and waited for one of them to speak.

"Where's she gonna stay? Here?" Tuck asked.

What? Rachel swung her eyes to Jake, ready to protest, but he beat her to it. "No, in a hotel closer to D.C. for now. She'll need to be near the Baltimore office during the investigation, and this way she'll be close to work if one of us needs to take her there for some reason."

She relaxed a little, glad that at least she wouldn't be intruding on them to that extent. "I'd prefer you run things past me and ask for my input before making decisions on my behalf," she said to Jake, wanting to make it clear that she wouldn't tolerate him dictating everything without at least talking to her.

He seemed to fight a smile at the edge in her tone, but nodded once. "Clay and I are training all day tomorrow, but if you need anything, Tuck can take care of it until I'm free," Jake told her.

She looked over at the others. "Thank you. I'm really sorry about any inconvenience this causes you guys, but I appreciate your help."

"Hey, no big deal," Tuck said, then looked at Clay and raised a pointed eyebrow at him. "Right?"

"Yeah," the big man grunted in a deep voice, though to her he sounded less than enthusiastic. She didn't blame him for feeling that way. He dealt with other people's crappy situations every day on the job, and here she'd just brought another one to their doorstep on their day off.

Jake spoke again. "The hotel will be secure enough, so you won't need one of us with you twenty-four seven, but if you need to leave it for any reason you should have one of us there just in case."

"Got it." Though she wished it could be just Jake who looked after her, she understood why he couldn't and was grateful that the others were willing to help look out for her. And hopefully this whole nightmare wouldn't last longer than a day or two more, because one: her head would explode, and two: a hotel for any longer than that would be crazy expensive and she didn't want to have to put a serious dent in her savings because of some asshole terrorizing her and her brother.

No, she told herself with a mental shake. Brandon would contact her, the FBI would catch Xang and she could go back to her life again. But there was something else she wanted to know.

"What about—" She stopped as her phone chimed with an incoming message.

Snatching it from the table, she read the text with her heart pounding, only to have it freeze in her chest as the words registered. She felt the blood rush out of her face, leaving her suddenly cold and woozy.

"What?" Jake demanded in a worried voice, leaning over to see the phone for himself.

Rachel automatically read the message once again, fear turning her insides to jelly as she realized that all this shit had just gotten far too real. "He's got Brandon," she rasped out, and shoved the phone at Jake.

Chapter Five

Letting himself into the hotel room a few hours later, Jake quietly closed the door behind him and met Rachel's gaze. His heart clenched at the sight of her red, swollen eyes.

She'd held it together from the time she'd received the chilling text and through the drive here to D.C., somehow managing to wait until he left to go talk to hotel security about the situation before finally venting her fear and grief in private. Normally the thought of comforting a crying woman made him uncomfortable as hell, but damn he wished he'd been here to hold Rachel.

That text had to be permanently burned into her brain, was probably all she could think about.

I have your brother. Bring me the blueprints tonight for every project you've worked on in the last three years. Come alone or he dies.

That was the gist of it. He'd also given explicit instructions on how and where the drop was to be made, and reiterated that Rachel was to come alone. If she brought cops or Feds with her, he'd kill Brandon. Jake knew that fear had been eating her alive ever since.

The analysts hadn't been able to verify that Xang had sent the message because he'd likely used a burner phone, so they couldn't trace or track it, and the clever bastard had even layered encryption shit on it. But it had to be him.

Xang might have slowed them down, but he hadn't won the war yet and he wouldn't get away with this. With the double whammy of being on the Most Wanted list and now the possible kidnapping on top of what he'd done in Rachel's place, Xang had just brought a large part of the FBI's manpower onto his case. He wouldn't be able to evade them much longer.

"Security's all up to speed on everything," Jake told Rachel, staying next to the door even though everything in him was dying for the chance to wrap his arms around her. "If they see anything suspicious they'll contact one of our guys. You're safe here."

She wiped her eyes, let out a hitching breath. "Thanks."

Ah, babe. He hated seeing her this way. "I've asked one of the agents at your place to pack you some stuff and bring it over. A female."

Rachel nodded. "I'd appreciate it."

To stem the urge to go to her, Jake shoved his hands into his jeans' pockets and leaned against the wall. "How you holding up?" He could see for himself, but he hoped she'd talk about it, let some of it out before she exploded.

She looked up at him with tormented eyes, as if to tell him what an asinine question it had been. "I'm freaking out and blaming myself for everything. If I'd handled things differently yesterday, maybe he would have listened, or at least he would have stayed the night at my place rather than with Tim—Xang—and the others. Then none of this would have happened."

Jake shook his head. "It's not your fault," he said firmly. "And Xang's not gonna do anything to him because he needs your brother as collateral until he gets what he wants from you." *I hope.* She flinched at his words and he silently cursed his bluntness. He pushed out a hard breath, unable to stand there and just watch her suffer. "What do you need right now?"

Her spine straightened, a hint of the fire inside her burning in her eyes. It heartened Jake to see it. She was gonna need every last bit of inner strength to see this through. "I need to know he's okay and to know exactly how the drop is going to go tonight."

They had no way of verifying whether her brother was all right, but he could at least ease her mind about the other. "The analysts are going to give you a copy of the plans to take to the drop, but slightly altered."

Her puffy eyes filled with alarm. "Altered how?"

He shrugged. "Just missing some precise details about entry and exit points, reinforcing structures, stuff like that. We can't give him the full schematics, for security reasons."

She came off the bed in a rush, fear radiating off her in a wave he could practically feel. "He'll hurt Brandon."

Jake held out a hand to stop her, make her listen. "We're going to take him down once you do the drop, so it won't matter because he won't get the chance to touch Brandon again. But even if he somehow transmits the plans to someone else before we move in, they'll look legit. We won't do anything to jeopardize Brandon or the lives of all those civilians potentially in the crossfire." Assuming Xang was planning some sort of terror attack on one of the buildings.

Rachel sucked in a deep, shaky breath and closed her eyes as though fighting for control, and Jake couldn't take it anymore. He covered the distance between them in two strides and pulled her into a tight hug.

A shiver ripped through her and she sighed, wrapping her arms around his back as she pressed her cheek to his chest. Jake closed his eyes too. It felt so good to have her in his arms, accepting the comfort he offered. He nuzzled the top of her head, breathed in the sweet scent of vanilla and warm woman.

Running a hand over the length of her slender back, he tried to reassure her about what was coming. "I'm gonna be as close to you as I can get tonight without being detected, and Tuck and Clay will be there too, along with an undercover team. You'll have an earpiece no one will be able to see, so we can hear you and you can hear us if we need to abort at the last second. We're gonna have you covered every step of the way, sweetheart."

He'd never allow her to make the drop otherwise. Would never have allowed her to participate period if her brother's life hadn't been in jeopardy. "And once you've made the drop and get out of range, we'll take him down."

She nodded, her cheek rubbing against his chest, seeming content to stay nestled in his embrace. And he sure as hell wasn't in any hurry to let her go. "But it won't be Xang who shows up."

Probably not, unless he was stupid or fucking desperate. The first wasn't likely. The second was a good bet, and it made him incredibly unpredictable and dangerous. "Then whoever it is will lead us to him. We'll get him and find your brother. It'll all be over soon."

"What if someone else comes for the designs and transmits them to Xang?" she said against his shirt. "How are we going to get proof of life?"

And that was the giant sinkhole in this plan the guys at the field office had come up with. He'd figured Rachel would see it from a mile away, and he'd been right. "He's a hacker, not a murderer." At least as far as they knew.

Another nod, but he could tell she wasn't convinced, and his words must have sounded just as hollow to her as they did to him. He just hoped the field office was right about that. "You'll get a full briefing of everything in a couple hours. We're not gonna leave anything to chance, least of all your safety."

"I know." She sighed, squeezed him once then pulled back to put some distance between them and Jake reluctantly released her. The wobbly little smile she gave him hit him straight in the heart. "Thanks, I needed that."

He reached out and wiped a trace of moisture from the top of her right cheek. "Anytime. You just let me know when you want another." Because he'd be more than happy for an excuse to hold her again. It tore him up inside to see her hurting like this.

She let out a soft laugh and he was glad to see that sparkle come back to her eyes. "I will. I've missed your hugs."

Right then he was having a hell of a time reminding himself why he shouldn't grab her and kiss her until she forgot everything but the feel of his mouth on hers, but the moment was shattered when his cell phone buzzed. A jolt of surprise hit him when he saw the familiar number. *Rycroft.* "Hey, man. How are you?" He hadn't seen him since Pakistan back in October.

"You know how it is. No rest for the wicked," Alex answered.

"I hear ya. And Grace?" She'd suffered direct exposure to the sarin gas during the last op to get Hassani. Minimal exposure, but still, that shit was no laughing matter.

"Grace is unbelievably amazing," Alex said, his voice laced with satisfaction. "Clean bill of health and docs don't need to see her for another three months until her next checkup. She said to say hi. But we'll catch up some other time because I'm calling about business. I hear you've got a bad personal situation going down."

Jake sighed and turned away slightly, aware that Rachel was watching him curiously. "You heard right. I was gonna call you about it tonight. How'd you hear about it?"

"Got a call from some Fed named Travers. He brought me up to speed. You need anything?"

That made Jake like Travers all the more. But besides granting a miracle that Brandon would still be alive when they found him, there was little that even someone as powerful and connected as Alex could do for them at this point. "Some extra eyes and ears would be good."

"Already on it. Zahra and some other linguists are looking into the Uyghur cell Xang's with, and hunting for any chatter about Brandon Granger's disappearance. If we find anything of use, I'll call you personally."

Knowing Alex and Zahra were monitoring the situation made him feel a bit better about things. "Thanks, man."

"You bet. Call me if you need anything else. I'll be in touch if I hear anything."

After he ended the call, Jake looked back at Rachel, who was still watching him. "That was Alex Rycroft, the NSA agent I worked with before. He's a big deal there, and in the intelligence community as a whole." As in, one of the *big* boys in that world. "He's got people working on Brandon's case, including an analyst I worked with before. She's one of the best. They'll call me if they find out anything, but he wanted me to know they're on it. Trust me when I say that's a very good thing."

"I'm grateful for any help they can give us."

Before he could say anything else, an abrupt knock sounded at the door.

Jake checked the peephole before opening it and letting the female agent in. "Rachel, this is Special Agent Celida Morales."

"I brought you some clothes," Morales announced to her, marching past Jake with a swish of her long, dark hair to set a small duffel on the bed. "I saw the labels on your stuff at your place and we dropped by the mall to grab something to eat on the way here, so I stopped in at Victoria's Secret to get you some new underwear while I was there."

Huh? "The agency paid for that?" Jake said in astonishment.

Morales cut him a bland look with her dark gray eyes. "Don't worry about who paid for it."

"I'll pay them back," Rachel said quickly, reaching for her purse.

"Pretty sure you can just give Morales the cash then," Jake said dryly, shaking his head at the agent. She liked to come across as such a hard ass, and she was on the job, but this just proved she was still a softie underneath.

Morales narrowed her eyes at him in a silent warning not to say anything more about it. "The store was on my way, so I thought it only right she get some of that pretty stuff replaced." She raised her eyebrows in a haughty gesture. "And you can leave now. I think you've seen more than enough of her underwear for one day, am I right?" She looked at Rachel, who swung her gaze to his, looking slightly uncomfortable at the thought of being left alone with the female agent.

Jake was still stuck back on the underwear thing. He'd seen what she wore strewn all over her room this morning. The thought of seeing Rachel in nothing but those bits of colored silk and lace shot a bolt of lust through his system. Mentally shaking himself, he changed the subject. "You okay if I go check in with the others for a bit?" he asked her.

"Sure. I need to call my mom anyway." She put her hands in her lap, the slight tension in her face telling him she was dreading that way more than she was letting on.

He couldn't help her with that and knew she wanted privacy for the call, so he nodded. "I've got my cell on me if you need me. I'll be back within a couple hours." He shifted his attention to Morales. "I appreciate this."

She waved his thanks away. "Don't worry about it. Been a while since I had some girl talk, and I'm sure Rachel could use a break from the toxic levels of testosterone she's been exposed to so far today. Right?" She nudged Rachel with an elbow.

Ignoring Morales, Rachel kept her eyes pinned on him. "You're coming back though, right?" Worry lurked in her eyes as she watched him.

That protective instinct he'd always felt with her flared up so hot and fast it was all he could do not to cross the room and haul her into his arms. "Yeah, as soon as we're done with the briefing." She seemed to relax at his words and he wished Morales wasn't there so he could wrap his arms around her tight and say a lot more, that he'd be here for her no matter what.

Instead he nodded at them both, left and started down the hall. Time was ticking down. Only a few more hours until the drop. Rachel was going to be a ball of nerves by then.

When he came back to get her, he would make sure they were alone so he was free to soothe her and say whatever the hell he wanted.

****

As it turned out, Agent Morales wasn't nearly as intimidating as first impressions would suggest.

When she'd first strode into the hotel room like

she'd owned the place and kicked Jake out, Rachel had been uncomfortable. But the woman had not only investigated at her place, she'd stopped at the mall and paid out of her own pocket to buy Rachel some new underwear on her way over. That thoughtful gesture meant a lot to her.

Knowing Xang had invaded her home and slashed her most intimate garments had shaken her more than she wanted to admit, or for Jake to know. But Agent Morales had known, and Rachel had a feeling that's why she'd gone to the trouble of specifically going to Victoria's Secret to get her new stuff.

And, after a few hours alone in her company, Rachel found the woman was friendly and amazingly easy to talk to. Several other agents had come up to brief her on what to expect tonight, and also what was expected *of* her, then she'd been left alone with Agent Morales again.

As the waiting period before the drop dragged on, Morales must have sensed how anxious Rachel had been, because she'd started asking her questions that had become more and more personal. At first it had seemed like a mini-interrogation of sorts, but then Rachel had quickly embraced the conversation, glad for the distraction.

Over the next two hours they'd talked over everything, including Jake. Normally she was a very private person, but Rachel had grown so comfortable with Morales that she'd found herself telling the woman certain details about their past.

Not admitting her true feelings for Jake or anything like that, merely talking about how they met at college and that they'd been dating other people. With everything that had happened since yesterday, it felt good to be able to open up and talk to another woman, even if she only gave small details. She had plenty of

MARKED

girlfriends, a few really close ones, but couldn't tell any of them about any of this until her brother was found and the investigation was over.

And if she was honest, she was curious and wanted to find out about Jake's life over the past few years from someone who'd known him during the time she'd missed out on.

"I don't know Jake all that well on a personal level," Morales said now, pushing her long, dark ponytail off her shoulder to trail down her back. She had the most interesting eyes—a deep, clear gray that stood out even more because of her light bronze skin tone. "But I do know he's a solid operator and a stand-up guy. Tuck and the other guys love him. Well, love is maybe not the right—you know what I mean."

Something about her expression as she mentioned the other man drew Rachel's attention. A slight softening. "You know Tuck as well?"

It was subtle, but Rachel noticed the agent broke eye contact as she answered. "Yep, we were partnered together once upon a time, worked some investigations early on before we went on to bigger and badder things." She shook her head fondly. "Agents have to serve two years as a Special Agent to hone their investigative skills before they can apply to HRT, so that's how that happened. Those guys, they live and breathe their job, which is good considering how demanding it is." Her smile faded and her gaze turned speculative as she focused on Rachel once more. "You think you could handle that? I mean, if you and Jake ever got together?"

Rachel ducked her head and rubbed the back of her neck, uncomfortable as hell in the face of such a direct and very personal question about her complex feelings for Jake. She chose her words with care. "Let's just say that if anything ever *did* happen—hypothetically," she qualified, "his job wouldn't be a problem for me. I know

83

that kind of lifestyle wouldn't be easy, but I'd make sure I was supportive. I know what making the team meant to him, and I know what staying on it means too. It's his dream."

Morales smiled and gave a satisfied nod, and Rachel felt like she'd just passed some sort of test. "Good to hear. Well," she said, rising in her sexy black suede pumps from where she'd been perched on the foot of the bed. "Anything else you wanna go over before I leave?"

"I can't think of anything else, except will you be working on my brother's case?"

"Absolutely. I work domestic terror cases so Xang's involvement means I'm all over this. You've got the A-Team behind you on this one." She gave Rachel's shoulder a firm pat. "Don't worry about the drop tonight. You'll do great. And aside from the rest of the team, Jake will be on you like your own personal shadow."

A knock on the door stopped Rachel from responding, but when Morales opened the door and Jake walked in, Rachel's heart leapt in her chest. His dark gaze zeroed right in on her, filling her with a sudden feminine awareness. Her nipples tightened and her pulse accelerated.

"How you doin', hon?" he asked, the endearment hitting her square in the chest. He used to call her that, toward the end of their final year in college. Back when they'd been close and wanting to be closer. "Morales been taking good care of you?"

"I've been amazingly pleasant and easy to be around, haven't I?" she said to Rachel. "And I already told her, it's Celida. None of this 'agent' stuff between us girls." She sauntered to the door, her full curves highlighted by the snug gray skirt suit she wore, a few shades lighter than her eyes. "You guys call me if you need anything." She shot a glance at Rachel over her shoulder. "You know, if you have any more uh…questions about anything." She gave a subtle tip of her head toward Jake and raised her eyebrows.

"I will," Rachel said with a smile. "Thanks for keeping me sane the past couple hours."

"My pleasure, doll. See ya 'round, farmboy." She popped Jake in the shoulder with a fist on her way out the door, hard enough to knock him sideways a few inches.

"I like her," Rachel announced after Jake shut the door. She felt light years better than before the visit.

"Yeah, she's pretty great, and a damn fine investigator according to Tuck." He put his hands into his pockets as he looked at her. "So, they told me they already brought you up to speed on everything about tonight. You ready for this?"

"Yes." More than anything she just wanted to hurry up and get it over with so they could get Brandon back safely. She knew what she was supposed to do, where she was to go, what to say if anyone suspicious approached or spoke to her. They'd been vague about the security detail accompanying her tonight, but she knew Jake would be there no matter what and that made her feel infinitely better about the whole thing.

Everything else was out of her control so she refused to allow herself to worry about it. "When do we leave?"

"Ten minutes."

"Oh." That had come up way faster than she'd expected. Nerves twisted her belly at the news.

His expression softened in understanding and he held out a hand to her. "Come here."

Something about the softly spoken command and the heat in his eyes as he gave it sent a shiver of primal awareness through her. She rose and walked over to him, aware of the pulsing silence in the room and the way her blood raced in her veins as he watched her. Jake waited until she'd halted a foot from him before reaching his hand up to stroke it over her hair, down to her left shoulder.

The gesture was both tender and intimate, the warmth of his fingers against her neck making her pulse jump. Gazing deep into her eyes, he brought his hand around in front of her and opened his fingers to reveal a tiny bit of plastic.

"Your earpiece," he murmured, tucking her hair behind her left ear as he held out the device for her. "Slide it in and tap it once to activate it."

She slid it into place and tapped it, watching him, fascinated by the heat in those dark eyes.

"Can you hear me?" he whispered, his voice barely carrying in the quiet, but it was amplified in her left ear. It felt intimate. Sensual. If he was trying to distract her from her anxiety, he was doing a hell of a good job.

She nodded, her mouth going dry as her gaze dropped to his lips. So close. What she wouldn't give to have them on hers right now. But she was already feeling off balance and vulnerable so she wasn't going to make the first move.

His mouth twitched slightly in a hint of a smile, as though he guessed what she'd been thinking. "Tap it twice." She did. "What about now?"

She shook her head, feeling strangely dizzy as she stared back at him. "It's off."

"Good." He took her face between his hands, his thumbs moving gently over her cheekbones, making sensitive nerve endings tingle. "When they drop you off you won't be able to see me, but I'll be close and so will the others. Nothing's gonna happen to you, I promise."

She swallowed, her throat tight from a mix of fear at what she was about to do and the aching need he ignited in her.

He shook her once gently, holding her gaze. "Say you believe me."

"I believe you." It came out a breathy whisper, an erotic invitation in the charged space between them. No way could she not kiss him. She swayed toward him, her body making the decision for her, her eyelids fluttering closed as he bent his head...

Abruptly he pulled back, his expression set as he tapped his earpiece. "Go." His eyes burned with unfulfilled desire and regret as he stared down at her and listened to whatever was being said. "Roger that. Be down in five." With a deep sigh, he smoothed a hand over her hair and set her away from him. "They're waiting for you."

Nodding because she didn't trust her voice yet, Rachel licked her lips. Her entire body was humming, craving that kiss, the taste of him, even as her heart pounded in terror of what she was about to do.

"Turn your earpiece on."

She started to shake her head, wanting to clear this up between them, find out exactly where they stood before she did the drop. Just in case. She couldn't stand the uncertainty a moment longer. Did he want more than friendship or not? "Not yet, I—"

He silenced her with a finger against her sensitive lips. A slow, sexy smile spread across his face and his eyes glowed. "Later. I promise we'll talk tonight after this is all done, okay? Right now I need you to have your game face on."

Her throat tightened as she realized he was telling her he did want more. How much more, she wasn't sure, but it was enough for now as long as she got a clearer answer later. "Okay."

His stare was so intense it smoldered. "Just remember we've got your back out there."

She knew Jake would do whatever it took to protect

her. "I know. And you be careful too."

"I will," he said, grinning as though her concern amused him.

She tapped her earpiece, struggling to find her balance now that he'd thrown her world off-kilter. "It's on."

"Okay." He took her hand, twined his fingers through hers and squeezed as he reached for the door. "You can do this, babe, no sweat. Now let's go get this done."

Chapter Six

The cool, damp night air washed over Rachel as she got out of the unmarked car and shut the door. She tugged her raincoat closer around her body to ward off the chill and resisted the urge to reach up and check her earpiece. Late afternoon rain showers had left puddles standing here and there on the pavement, the water reflecting the brightly colored lights from the lamps and signs overhead.

The driver, an undercover FBI agent, pulled away immediately, leaving her alone on the corner near the entrance to Chinatown. They'd given her a tracking device that she'd attached to the back of one of her earrings. That and the earpiece still weren't enough to settle the nerves fizzing in her belly.

Pulling the collar of her leather jacket up higher to block the chilly breeze, she walked toward the ornate red gates that marked the entrance of Chinatown, her shoes making wet slapping sounds on the damp pavement. Being a Saturday night, the area was busy, packed with cars and pedestrians going to the night market and the many shops and restaurants in the district. Her destination was one of the stalls set up at the market, a few blocks away.

Hands tucked into her jacket pockets, she curled the fingers of her right hand around the USB drive one of the analysts had given her that contained the altered files. They'd assured her time and time again that the files were complete enough that the tampering wouldn't be detected even if the information was somehow transmitted before the team could move in and arrest whoever picked it up—assuming Xang wasn't a total whacko and actually showed up himself tonight.

They'd better be right about that, because right now no one had a clue where Brandon might be.

They also assumed that whoever came to pick up the files wasn't actually going to meet Xang in person, since that would only lead anyone following the runner straight to him. Once the agents made the arrest, they planned to find out how the person was going to transmit the files to Xang and duplicate the method exactly, thereby getting a starting point to begin the search for him and Brandon.

Her pulse thudded in her throat. Telling herself to stay calm, she crossed the street and entered the tall gates with their sculpted Chinese lions flanking either side, following the instructions Jake and the others had given her.

Walk tall. Head up. Don't glance around like you're expecting to be watched. Don't look for us. We'll be there.

Even though there were plenty of people around and she knew the undercover agents were out there somewhere, she still felt nervous and exposed out here.

Jake's voice came through her earpiece. "You're doing great. Scratch your nose if you hear me."

She did, resisting the urge to look around for him in the shadows. And she knew better than to say anything in reply, in case she was being watched or followed by whoever Xang had sent.

"Perfect. Tuck and I have you covered and everyone else is in position. You'll be just fine."

It helped to hear his voice and know he could see her even if she couldn't see him. If anything happened, he'd be there to help. She pushed out a breath and continued down the sidewalk past steamy windows of restaurants serving hand-pulled noodles and genuine Cantonese or Mandarin specialties.

The market always drew a lot of interest, including people outside the Chinese community who wanted a more authentic experience of Chinese cuisine and culture. The smell of barbecued pork and steamed dumplings wafted in the air as she turned right at the first corner and headed for the lit display tents set up in the market area.

When she was within forty feet of the stall she'd been told to make the drop at, the back of her neck prickled. Forcing back the urge to glance around, she waited in line at the food stall. Someone was watching her, she felt it.

Rachel stared straight ahead, watching people order and pay for their steamed buns and spicy shrimp. She was too nervous to be hungry, even with the tempting smells around her, but when it was her turn she ordered herself some sweet pork buns anyway.

The woman at the cash register took her money, filled the order and handed over a small cardboard takeout tray full of steamed buns. As Rachel accepted it, she quickly slipped the USB drive out of her pocket and placed it on the counter to the left of the register as she'd been told, then turned and began to walk away.

The prickling at her nape continued and this time it was impossible to keep from darting looks around for possible threats. Brandon's safety depended on this going down smoothly and she didn't want any screw-ups. To signal to the team that she'd successfully made the drop, she picked up a bun and forced herself to take a bite. The spiced meat and the dough felt heavy in her mouth but she made herself swallow it and keep walking, ignoring the hard thud of her heart.

She was almost at the end of the line of people waiting to order when out of the corner of her eye she noticed someone barreling toward her. Her stride faltered and she turned her head, eyes widening when she saw a man in a black hoodie coming straight for her. For an instant, panic seized her, rooting her in place.

"Rachel, run for the secondary extraction point," Jake commanded.

She whirled, bouncing off someone in the crowd as she tried to get away. Expecting to feel hands grabbing her from behind at any second, she was surprised when the man coming her way blew past her, headed for the stall.

"*Run*," Jake barked. "We're moving in on them."

Them? Shoving her way through the knot of people surrounding her, she caught sight of two more men also dressed in black hoodies running toward her, pushing their way past people to clear the way.

She was outta there.

Praying Jake and the others would get them, Rachel burst out of the crowd and took off back the way she'd come. Half expecting someone to grab her, she veered left at the next corner and raced toward where the getaway car was supposed to show up.

****

Jake stayed back a few precious seconds longer to ensure Rachel made it to where a fellow agent had pulled the car up, then bolted from his position after the third suspect.

"Tuck, Bauer, report." Up ahead, the man Jake was

after darted around a corner. Bastard was fast, Jake would give him that. He dodged people as he raced after him, never taking his eyes off the back of that black hoodie.

"One just ducked into a restaurant up ahead," Tuck replied. "He's mine."

"Gaining on mine," Bauer said, his heavy breathing telling Jake he was still in hot pursuit.

Jake knew other agents were converging on the area right now but it was up to the three of them to at least keep a visual of the suspects. He planned to do a lot more than that. His boots pounded against the pavement with each racing stride. Helluva way for him and his buddies to spend their day off, but at least he knew Rachel was safe. Now, they were gonna nail the sons of bitches who'd come for that USB drive.

Halfway up the next block the guy tried and failed to leap over two people carrying what looked like a small couch. He caught his foot on the top of the thing and sailed headfirst over it, hitting the ground hard.

Those few seconds it took for him to scramble to his feet were all Jake needed. The suspect had just gained his footing and taken a lurching stride up the sidewalk when Jake caught him in a flying tackle. They hit the ground hard, the guy beneath him taking the full brunt of the impact, the breath rushing out of him in a loud, painful grunt. People cried out and scrambled away from them in surprise.

"FBI," Jake called out as he pinned the guy in place. "Stay back!"

Nobody moved as he flipped the man onto his stomach and seized his wrists, wrenching them behind his back before securing them with a plastic zip-tie. Once he was immobilized, Jake turned him back over again, not surprised to see an unfamiliar face staring up at him. He was in his late teens or early twenties, definitely of Asian descent, and his nose and chin were bleeding from their introduction to the pavement.

"Who are you," Jake growled, wasting no time in searching him. The kid didn't answer as he checked the pockets of the jacket and jeans. Jake found no weapons, and unfortunately no USB drive either. The only thing the guy had on him was a cell phone, which Jake took for further analysis.

Via the earpiece he reported his location to the rest of the team. "What's your name?" he demanded again, growing impatient. He wanted fucking answers, so they could get mobilized and rescue Rachel's brother, then bring Xang down.

He got nothing but an angry glare in response. Didn't much matter. The team would have portable biometric scanners to immediately upload his picture and fingerprints to AFIS and IDENT systems, so if this guy had a criminal history, they'd know about it pretty damn quick.

"Tuck?" he said instead, looking up to scan the immediate area. Two agents were running toward him. Jake stood guard over the suspect in case he got it in his head to try to get up and make another run for it.

"Got him," Tuck panted and gave his location, about three blocks east of Jake. "Unarmed, and no sign of the files."

"Got mine too," Bauer reported a moment later, sounding out of breath. "I'm four blocks northwest of you, Evers. Little bastard ducked into a restaurant and convinced the owners to hide him in their apartment upstairs. He was trying to climb out the fire escape in back when I got there."

"Has he got the files?" Jake asked.

"Negative, but he's got a cell on him and some other stuff."

They'd seen the first guy grab the USB from the

food stand, but it was likely he'd passed it off to one of the others when he'd realized they were being chased. "I'm moving to you now." Jake waited for the other agents to come over and take charge of the suspect before jogging up to Bauer's position.

He found the former SEAL towering over the prisoner cuffed face-down on the floor of the tiny restaurant. Someone had ushered all the patrons out into the street, but the older man and woman who Jake assumed were the owners stood huddled together behind the counter, watching the proceedings with wide eyes.

Jake pulled out his ID and held it up for them to see before looking at what Bauer held in his gloved hands. A cell phone and some kind of electronic transmitter.

"I can't get in," Bauer said. "Password protected and he's not cooperating."

Wouldn't take their analysts long to get what they needed. Jake went down on one knee beside the suspect. Young Asian male, probably in his early twenties. "Who are you?"

"Michael," the kid answered in a heavy accent.

"Michael who?"

"Michael Wong."

"What were you doing in the market tonight, Mike?"

"Getting food."

Riiiight. "So why'd you run from us?"

Mike rolled his head enough to glower at Jake. "He chasing me," he said, jerking his chin at Bauer.

Yeah, seeing a two-hundred-thirty pound wall of muscle and bad attitude charging after you would make most people run in the opposite direction, but Michael was fucking lying and they all knew it.

"What's this for?" Jake held out the electronic thingy and the cords connected to it. He bet the kid had no clue when he took this job that the FBI would show up to bust him tonight.

"My phone." But now he was avoiding eye contact and his face was slowly turning red.

Jake opened his mouth to blast him but stopped when three agents wearing FBI windbreakers entered the restaurant. One of them held up a plastic evidence bag. "Found this outside in the back alley," he said, showing Jake the USB drive Rachel had left next to the cash register.

"What were you doing with it?" Jake demanded, glaring down at Michael.

"Nothing. Not mine."

Stupid fucker wasn't even wearing gloves so they'd be able to pull prints off it if necessary. "He must have connected to it with this," he told the agent, holding out the device Bauer had found.

Jake moved back as the other agents took over, hauling Michael to his feet and reading him his rights while they escorted him out of the restaurant. Tuck showed up just as they were all leaving. "You find the USB drive?"

"Yeah, but there's a possibility he somehow transmitted the files to Xang."

"Ah, hell. You gonna tell Rachel?"

"Yeah." He was gonna have to. She'd been so worried about what Xang would do if the plans had been tampered with, and they'd all assured her it would never be a concern because they'd get him long before he could use the information. That plan had rapidly wound up in the shitter. She deserved to hear it from him, but she was likely going to freak when she found out. He'd wait until the analysts confirmed it first though. Goddammit.

"Thanks for the help, boys," he said to Tuck and Bauer.

"Anytime," Tuck said with a grin. "Nothing like a

little chase and takedown in an urban area to get the blood pumping on a Saturday night."

"Not quite as good as dirt biking," Bauer interjected.

"Oh, of course not," Jake agreed with a chuckle. "Let's head back and give our reports so you guys can take off for the night."

"I'd be happy to stay after and talk to Rachel for you," Tuck offered.

Jake shot him a hard look, conveying without words that Rachel was off limits. "Not a chance."

Tuck shrugged and tried to hide a grin. "Can't blame a guy for trying."

"Yeah, I can, actually."

Laughing, Tuck led the way out into the cool spring air.

After giving their reports the guys headed home but Jake stayed behind to await the analysts' findings. He waited another forty minutes until Agent Travers finally came out to give him an update.

"The kid definitely e-mailed the contents to someone," Travers said. "We're trying to figure out how much of it actually got through before he chucked the USB drive out the window when he heard Bauer coming. Looks like the account he sent it to is new. We're tracing it but we think everything's been encrypted on the other end because so far we can't trace anything."

Jake ran a hand over his face. He wasn't looking forward to relaying this to Rachel. "What's the link to Xang?"

"Preliminary reports suggest they were all low-level gang members, or possibly wannabes trying to be initiated or earn some street cred. Xang apparently approached them this afternoon with the offer of money for pulling off the job. They all knew they'd have to compete against two others on the job, so the first person there was to pick up the USB drive and transmit its contents to the e-mail address they were given. You and I both know it was Xang. We just can't prove it yet."

And meanwhile Rachel's brother was still being held prisoner somewhere. "When will you know about the files?"

"Could be an hour, might be a couple days."

They didn't have a couple days. If Xang was this desperate to get the plans, there was no telling how unpredictable he might be with a live hostage. Travers knew it as well as Jake did.

"All right. You'll let me know if you find anything more?"

"You know it." He slapped a hand on Jake's back. "Morales is with Rachel at the hotel right now. Just tell her we're on top of it and doing everything we can."

"Sure." It wasn't going to do shit to ease her mind, but he wasn't going to lie to her to make her feel better. He just hoped this botched attempt to locate Xang didn't ruin her trust in him and kill what was building between them before it even had a chance to happen.

Chapter Seven

Reclining on the bed in her hotel room, Rachel shot up straight when someone knocked on the door. Celida checked the peephole and spoke as she reached for the doorknob. "It's Jake."

Rachel stood as he entered, trying to read his face for clues but his expression was blank. Whatever had happened, it wasn't good news. She knew he would have called her if they'd found Brandon. A rush of panic swept through her.

Forcing it back, she found her voice. *Tell me I'm wrong. Tell me everything's fine and that you got him.* "Hi."

"Hey." His gaze shifted to Celida. "You going to the meeting at the office?"

"Yeah," she said dryly, "but that wasn't very subtle of you. It's okay though—I can tell when I'm not wanted anymore." She shot what was probably supposed to be an encouraging smile at Rachel. "Later."

Rachel murmured a goodbye as Celida walked into the hall. The moment the door shut behind her, Rachel turned to Jake. "What happened?" she demanded. "Did you find out anything about Brandon? Where he is, or if he's okay?" Her heart thudded a hard, desperate rhythm against her ribs. They had to know something concrete by now.

Jake shook his head and Rachel's heart sank like a chunk of lead. "Did Morales update you at all?"

Dread swelled, eroding the disappointment. "No. She took a phone call before you got here, but she didn't tell me anything about what was said. Please tell me what's going on."

He sighed and began stripping off his jacket. "There were three guys at the drop. We arrested them all, and one of them had the USB. Best we can tell, he managed to e-mail the files to someone."

No. "Xang?" she managed, trying not to freak out.

He tossed the jacket over the back of a chair. "We think so. They're working on it right now."

Oh my God. This was what she'd feared about dropping the altered files.

She put a hand on her forehead. "So basically you're telling me we have no idea where he is, if he's still got Brandon, and whether my brother's still alive or not." Okay, the trying not to freak out thing wasn't working. She was too stressed out, too terrified for Brandon.

To his credit, Jake didn't look away or try to blow off her concern. "Yeah. I'm sorry."

Rachel turned away, dragging her hands through her hair as she struggled to keep from letting the anger and terror swamp her. Her heart hammered against her ribs. She wanted to hit something. Throw something. "God, I *knew* this would happen—"

"If it did go to Xang, then he's got what he wants."

He wasn't seriously suggesting that Xang might let Brandon go, was he? Brandon was a witness. Xang would likely kill him for that alone and Jake knew it as well as she did.

She dropped her hands and whirled to face him,

pinning him with a hot glare, aware that she was close to coming unglued and not caring that he was a convenient target. "Until he finds out the files aren't complete. *Then* he'll sure as hell have a reason to kill Brandon if he hasn't already, won't he?"

Again, Jake didn't flinch at her anger or try to dodge the accusation. "Now they've got a more solid starting place to track him. They'll find him *and* your brother."

She turned away again, shaking her head as she moved to the window. Below them the lights of the business district glinted off the wet pavement, while she felt trapped in darkness. "But will they find him in time?" Her voice cracked on the last word, her tenuous hold on her emotions slipping.

Quiet footfalls behind her warned of his approach. She didn't turn, just kept staring out the window so he wouldn't see how close she was to crying.

She felt the heat of him against her back an instant before his warm, strong hands settled on her hips. His fingers flexed. "They will."

He sounded so sure but she wasn't convinced. Rachel swallowed, tried to speak past the restriction in her throat. "He's the only brother I have." Her only sibling, and the only family she had here in the States.

"I know he is. You can't give up hope. I need you to keep believing for him."

She wanted to yell at him that it fucking hurt to feel this scared, so scared it made her feel physically ill. But none of this was Jake's fault and he was only trying to help. Hell, he'd dropped everything and put himself in harm's way tonight to help. Dammit, she just wanted to hear Brandon's voice at least, hear that he was still alive.

When she still didn't turn, Jake simply slid his arms around her waist from behind and eased her back to rest against his chest. Rachel stiffened, resisting the embrace.

She knew he'd meant to comfort her but all it did was push her closer to tears, both from her worry about Brandon and the torture of feeling that hard, lean body at her back.

"You did good tonight," he murmured against the top of her head, her hair snagging on his beard.

She snorted. "I walked up to a food counter and put down a memory stick. Big deal." And she'd been scared the whole time, even with a freaking FBI team there to back her up. God, and to think how terrified Brandon must be right now on his own wherever Xang had taken him.

"Hey." Jake tightened his arms, jerking her out of her thoughts and making her extremely aware of the muscles caging her so protectively.

A volatile mix of anger, frustration and need warred inside her. She was so torn, part of her wanting what he was tempting her with—the chance to finally feel his mouth, hands and body all over her after all this time—but the timing made her conscience squirm. What kind of person got turned on when their only sibling was being held hostage, for God's sake?

Jake's calm, steady voice spoke close to her ear. "Blaming yourself isn't going to find him any faster."

The need to lash out at something was strong, but the feel of Jake cradling her this way was quickly transforming that need into something hotter, more primal. She was keyed up inside, all her anxiety and frustration looking for an outlet. "Maybe not, but it's making me feel better at the moment."

"I'd rather make you feel better another way."

There was no mistaking the sensual tone in his deep voice.

In the silence that followed, she was intensely aware that they were alone behind a locked door. Jake's body was so warm and solid as he cradled her. Offering her the very solace she yearned for more than anything, a way to push everything else away for a little while. He could have gotten hurt or worse tonight, but he'd gone in without hesitation to help her. Her breasts felt tight and swollen, an empty ache blooming between her thighs where a slick heat gathered.

"I'm glad you're okay," she murmured. Even knowing what he did for a living hadn't eased her worry any when she'd caught sight of him sprinting toward the man she'd run from in the market.

"It was fine, the suspects weren't even armed."

Before she could respond she felt him nuzzle the back of her hair. Goosebumps raced across her skin. Her nipples beaded tight as warmth permeated her body. She sucked in a breath, every muscle tightening in anticipation. Jake pushed her hair aside with his nose and nuzzled her sensitive nape, his warm breath teasing her, all those whiskers prickling gently.

She closed her eyes as desire slid through her, warring with the frustration, the overwhelming fear. "Jake..."

He'd said they'd talk about things once the drop was done, and even though his actions were making it more than clear about what he wanted, she needed to hear the words. But as much as she wanted him in return, the idea of having sex while Brandon was suffering was just plain wrong.

"Turn around," he whispered against her skin, his lips grazing her hairline. She shivered at the underlying command in his voice.

Those strong, capable hands slid to her waist, gripped her gently while his fingers flexed, giving her a mere hint of the hunger inside him. Waiting. More than willing to give her the oblivion her body craved, even if it was only a temporary reprieve.

She leaned harder against him, his patience and

consideration of her feelings undid her. Maybe she deserved to go to hell for wanting to jump this man while her brother was a hostage, but there was no way she could walk away from Jake and the outlet he offered now.

Slowly she turned and looked up into his eyes. He kept his hands on her waist, his thumbs stroking in distracting little patterns against the sides of her belly that sent tendrils of pleasure twining down to the building throb between her legs.

"The agency's doing everything it can. You've done everything *you* can. That's gonna have to be enough for right now," he said as he lifted a hand and brushed the hair back from her cheek. The look in his eyes was so full of tenderness and need it caused a flipping sensation in her belly.

She heard the wisdom in his words, but wanted to be clear on his motive. She caught his wrist, wrapped her fingers around it and felt the tendons flex beneath her fingers. So strong, so solid. "If you're doing this just to distract me, don't."

It came out more a plea than a warning. She couldn't stand the thought of him doing this out of pity or a misguided effort to take her mind off Brandon. The emotional stakes were too high for her. She'd held back her true feelings for him for so long, in deference to him and Linda. If they crossed the line from friends to lovers, it had to mean more to him too because there was no going back and she wasn't willing to have him once only to lose him later.

His expression softened, but the flare of heat in his eyes burned hotter. "Trust me, that's not even close, babe." Keeping his hand in her hair, that dark-chocolate gaze dipped to her mouth, then back up to her eyes. The air between them crackled with pent-up sexual tension. She stared up at him, watched in fascination as his pupils expanded to swallow the dark brown irises and an answering wave of desire rushed through her.

She wanted to attack that mouth just inches above her own. Vent the anger and longing and desire she'd held back for so long.

Part of her still couldn't believe that Jake was actually holding her the way she'd always wanted, his expression full of a hunger that made all of her hot spots ache.

She gripped his broad shoulders, breathless at the feel of the muscles bunching beneath her fingers. All that power coiled there under her hands, held in check, used to seduce and protect rather than take. Her knees went a little weak. She'd waited for him after he'd broken up with Linda, keeping in e-mail contact in the hopes that he'd come to her. When he hadn't she'd forced herself to cut ties and move forward because she couldn't stand to be *just* his friend. She couldn't. It had slowly been killing her.

"I wanted to wait," he began, sounding almost regretful as he stared into her eyes, "but I feel like I've waited forever for you already, so fuck if I'm gonna wait a second longer." His hand tightened in her hair, gripping it in his fist as he tipped her head back.

Her sharply indrawn breath seemed to echo between them. His eyes turned even darker as he bent his head and slammed his mouth down on hers. Rachel met the kiss with every ounce of pent-up need and frustration inside her, pressing up on tiptoe to take what he offered.

Jake made a dark, hungry sound at the back of his throat, slanting his lips across hers, the kiss so raw and intense that she moaned. They fed from each other, unleashing the raging hunger between them. She trembled at the sheer power of it. Tingles raced throughout her body, the pleasure already so sharp it was a sweet torture.

Jake suddenly slowed the ravenous pace. He licked at her lower lip instead, a seductive caress, ignoring the way she opened in invitation, seeming to savor teasing her. Rachel mewled in frustration, needing so much more from him, her fingers biting into the muscle bunching beneath her hands.

His hold tightened, his right arm a band of steel across her lower back as he pushed his tongue between her lips to taste her. He absorbed her gasp, the hand at her back sliding up to splay between her shoulder blades as he licked and caressed.

God, the man could kiss. She was already breathless, floating, desperate to get naked and feel his skin on hers, feel him plunge into her.

Rachel whimpered as he dragged her closer still and his tongue stroked every sensitive spot inside her mouth. His beard prickled her slightly, in sharp contrast to the silky smoothness of his lips and tongue. He feathered teasing little touches against the tender roof of her mouth, slid it against hers in a seductive caress that made her ache to have him inside her.

She flattened her body against his to relieve the ache in her breasts and in her sex, meeting each stroke of his tongue, lost in the feel and taste of him. His fist released her hair to cup the back of her head and hold her steady, the other sweeping down her back to grip the curve of her ass. He made a low sound of pleasure as her belly came into solid contact with the hard ridge of his erection straining the front of his jeans.

She felt drunk on him, drowning in sensation and desire and didn't care if she never came up for air again.

All she could do was moan to convey the agonizing need inside her, but then Jake stiffened and jerked his head back. She leaned back, grateful for the strong arm around her back to keep her from falling as he let out a frustrated breath and reached up to tap his earpiece.

"Evers."

His eyes stayed on hers while whoever it was spoke to him. The burning hunger she saw reflected there was quickly banked by whatever was said. A muscle in his jaw flexed and a new tension filled his powerful frame. "Roger that," he said. "Be there in fifteen."

Tapping the earpiece again so that no one could overhear them, he sighed and eased his hold. "Babe, I gotta go back in."

She searched his eyes. "Everything okay?"

He nodded. "It's fine. They're just working some new intel and want me there at the briefing."

She knew he was being purposely evasive, but she also knew he'd tell her if it was something important. He wasn't officially part of the taskforce on Brandon's case, he'd only volunteered to help out at the drop tonight and she suspected they'd let him because he was an HRT member.

Running her hands over his shoulders once gently, already anticipating when she'd be able to do the same over his naked skin while he was buried deep inside her, she lowered her arms and stepped back. Instantly she felt colder, more alone. "Will I see you again tomorrow?"

His lips curved in a slow smile. Lips she couldn't wait to taste again. "Of course you will. I train all day but I'll come by as soon as I'm done."

She had no idea what she was supposed to do with herself in the meantime, but that wasn't his problem and he'd already gone above and beyond to help her. But God, she wished he would stay the night and just hold her in the darkness so she didn't feel so alone with her thoughts. "Okay. I'll see you tomorrow then."

His stare was hot enough to burn. "You can count on it. I'll check my phone when I can, but if you need anything call Morales or Tuck." He stroked his hand over the side of her face. "Try to get some sleep, and hang in there."

"I'll try my best."

His eyes crinkled at the corners as he smiled. "I know you will, and that'll be more than enough." He leaned down to give her a quick, hard kiss then grabbed his jacket and walked out of the room.

****

Xang wiped the back of his hand across his upper lip as he pulled the ringing phone out of his pocket. It felt like it was a hundred degrees in this old warehouse when it was probably closer to sixty.

He couldn't stop sweating, couldn't control the staccato beat of his heart. The op had almost been a disaster. "Did you get them?"

"They're incomplete," his contact spat back in Mandarin.

Xang blanched, suddenly feeling like he'd been dropped into a tub full of ice water. "What do you mean? That's impossible, I saw the plans myself." Had something gone wrong during the transfer? Had there been some kind of virus attached to the files he'd failed to notice?

"That's because you're completely ignorant about architecture," the man snapped. "There are layout features missing, measurements and dimensions missing."

"Does it affect the op?" Xang asked, trying to tamp down his growing fear.

"Of course it affects the op! You know how tight the timeline is. We have no choice but to go forward with what we have and the people already in place. The FBI will act quickly—we have to carry out the attack in the next forty-eight hours, otherwise we'll have no choice but to abort the entire thing."

Xang wiped at his damp face. They'd blame him for this. They couldn't track him here—not yet—so he still had some time if he ditched the burner phone, but damn. "I'll see if I can get the original plans on my own."

"Don't bother. You've done enough," the man said in a scathing tone. "Just know that if this attack fails, it'll be on your head."

Meaning if this glitch forced them to abort the attack, he was a dead man.

The line went dead before Xang could say anything else. With a shaking hand he threw the burner phone onto the ground and crushed it beneath the sole of his boot. There. That would buy him at least a few hours' head start to find a new hideout. He wasn't their lapdog, trained to blindly obey and come to heel when called. He had the resources, men who respected him and were loyal to him.

Xang knew he had to finish this on his own. He paced around the room, his footsteps echoing hollowly off the concrete walls.

He hadn't gone to the drop area in person because that would have been stupid, but he'd watched everything unfold with the help of CCTVs he'd hacked into in the area. He'd seen Rachel appear and leave the USB. He'd seen his hired men approach. Then the men chasing them through Chinatown. He knew damn well they'd been undercover Feds.

That bitch, he thought, raking his hands through his hair. Not only had she brought law enforcement with her when he'd specifically warned her what would happen if she did, she'd altered the files, made him look like an idiot *and* jeopardized the entire operation. And since he hadn't heard from any of the three guys he'd enlisted for the job, other than the initial e-mail transmitting the files, he knew they must still be in custody.

Xang's muscles knotted as he battled the rage

swamping him. He'd fucking *warned* her of the consequences. Did she not believe he'd actually kill her brother? That he didn't have the balls to go through with it? He'd killed before and he'd do it again.

The rage roared through him in a red tide, hazing his vision and making his heart pound. She deserved to lose her brother for that. And she deserved to die as well. Images of her dying at his hand flooded his mind, fueling the need for vengeance.

Once he got his hands on her he would kill her and whoever was guarding her. He might not be able to get to her right now, but he would teach her a lesson in the meantime, show her he was not to be fucked with.

He sucked in an unsteady breath, making a half-hearted attempt to stem the fury thrumming through him. Spinning on his heel, he stalked to the far end of the building where a closed door lay between him and his prisoner.

Throwing the steel door wide, it clanged against the wall to reveal the figure bound on his side to the wooden pallet. Brandon blinked as the light from the main part of the warehouse hit him, his face pinched with fear behind the gag as he held Xang's gaze.

"Your sister fucked everything up," he snarled, taking a menacing step toward him.

Brandon tried to shrink away but there was nowhere for him to go with the nylon ropes holding him in place. Xang took great pleasure in slowly reaching down to withdraw the knife from the sheath on his calf and holding it up so the light glinted off the wicked blade.

Brandon made a choked sound and shook his head frantically.

Xang felt the surge of power and excitement whip through his veins, erasing the fear and anger. He thought of the pictures he'd seen of his father and brother, their bodies mutilated and burned nearly beyond recognition as a warning to others who defied the Chinese government. Their fingernails and toenails had been pulled out first. The photos had shown the scabs forming over the raw wounds, so he knew it had been done first, before the digits had been cut off, one by one. Next, their sadistic captors had cut out their tongues and gouged their eyes from their sockets.

According to other prisoners who'd seen the torture and returned to the village after, his father and brother had still been alive when they'd been disemboweled and burned all over with branding irons. The Communist party hammer and sickle symbol had been seared into what little flesh remained.

Xang focused on his knife, the blade so clear and bright he could see his own reflection in the steel. His father's eyes stared back at him, demanding vengeance. Retribution. Starting with this.

"I'm going to let her know exactly what I think of that," he said to his prisoner before bending down and reaching for Brandon's bound hands.

Chapter Eight

C elida sat up straight in her chair to stretch the muscles in her neck and shoulders. "Whaddya think?" she asked Rachel, bent over the file between them. They were in her office at the Baltimore field office.

"I think that's everything."

Celida grunted in agreement and shoved the handwritten notes they'd compiled into the file. It was already dinner time and they'd been working for the past five hours solid without a break.

Of all the buildings Rachel had worked on since joining her architectural firm, a handful had been flagged for further analysis. Some located in or near Chinatown itself, others financed or owned by Chinese businesses. Analysts were running intel on them all now, looking at resident and guest lists, upcoming events that might be of interest to the radical group Xang had been recruited into.

"I'm done," she said, pushing back from her desk. "You hungry?" They hadn't stopped for lunch, so the last thing she'd eaten was a fruit tray and some yogurt in her hotel room this morning around five.

"I could eat." Rachel's expression said otherwise,

but the fact was, the woman needed to eat something. She was thin enough as it was. She needed to take care of herself or the stress was gonna take a serious toll on her body. They'd been poring over the blueprints and floor plans of all the flagged buildings, looking for possible concerns. Stress points, vulnerable areas, that kind of thing.

"Come on, let's get outta here and—" Celida stopped, practically froze in the act of rising from her chair as the door to her office opened to reveal Tuck standing between the jambs. His reaction was a bit subtler, but Celida saw the way he tensed a little when he saw her. "What are you doing here?" she blurted, frowning at him.

Those warm brown eyes held hers, calm and unreadable. "Came to hang with Rachel for a bit until farmboy can make it here."

Oh, that deep, honeyed drawl. Still so damn sexy. Annoyed, she pushed to her feet, unable to curb her knee-jerk defensiveness that his sudden appearance triggered. "She's hanging with me." She didn't need him to take over.

He stared back at her, his lips twitching a little as he tried to hide a smile. It was so unfair, what his smiles did to her. Way worse that he knew it. But at least she knew from the raw male interest in his eyes that she affected him just as much.

Which was why she raised an eyebrow in defiance and refused to look away, aware that Rachel was looking back and forth between them as they confronted each other for a few heartbeats of silence.

A very electric, charged silence, crackling with the possibility of what could have been. Could still be, if he wasn't so stubborn.

Rachel cleared her throat. "Um, I don't really need to eat—"

"Yes you do," Celida told her, finally peeling her eyes off Tuck long enough to shoot her an annoyed look. Damn the man, for showing up unannounced and throwing her off her calm, cool and collected game. She prided herself on it. "I know you're tired and you need to eat something."

"I just meant that I'm fine here on my own, or back at the hotel. You guys don't have to babysit me, I can fend for myself and there are more agents posted at the hotel. I'm more or less in protective custody anyway so it's not like I'd leave the hotel on my own."

And that was just one of the reasons why Celida already liked her so much. Rachel didn't bullshit and was a helluva lot more intelligent than most of the people she'd been assigned to protect over the course of her career.

"Nope. Sorry, no can do." Besides, she was a friend of Jake's—and if she wasn't mistaken, Rachel meant a whole lot more to him than just an old college buddy. If the jackass would get over himself already and admit he wanted to be more than friends.

God, Celida could *so* relate. Well, except that she and Tuck weren't exactly friends anymore.

In fact, they hadn't seen each other much since he'd made the HRT and left investigative work for good almost two years ago. Which was a damn shame. They'd been good together. Would be freaking *awesome* in bed if he'd just get over himself already.

"We'll both take her to eat," Tuck said by way of compromise, keys dangling from one broad, tan hand and his sunglasses from the other. Mother of Christ, the man was mouthwatering. Maybe not classically handsome, especially with all the knocks and nicks his face had suffered over the years, but to her he was by far the hottest man on the face of the earth.

And also the most pig-headed. That should have

killed some of the lust he inspired in her, but dammit, for some reason it just made her want him more. She couldn't resist the challenge.

And that air of absolute confidence he carried combined along with that hard body and the slow "oh-the-things-I'd-do-to-you-if-I-ever-got-you-naked" smile he sometimes gave her...yeah, she'd given up trying to get over him a long time ago. Even with all his goddamn irritating-as-shit mixed signals that even the FBI's best cryptologist wouldn't be able to decipher.

Pushing all those distracting thoughts away, she focused on Tuck, determined not to let him see how much he affected her. He got a kick out of flirting with her, teasing her with the promise of all she couldn't have and wasn't interested in moving out of the friend-zone.

Fine. She hadn't spent this much time in the testosterone-laced environment of the Marine Corps and then the FBI not to recognize that giving a man like him that much power would be epically stupid. Something she'd learned early on in life. She could absolutely do dinner with him and Rachel and pretend she felt nothing. See how he liked that.

"Fine. But one of us will need to stay back at the hotel with her after until—" She broke off when Travers suddenly appeared in the doorway next to Tuck, the top of the agent's slightly graying head barely reaching Tuck's nose.

"Am I interrupting anything important?" Travers asked, glancing between them.

"No," Celida answered, more forcefully than she'd intended. "We were just going to take Rachel out to grab a bite to eat. She's been very helpful with the investigation so far. We don't want her fading away on us."

Travers turned his attention to Rachel, who'd risen and was standing uncertainly on the other side of the table. "Before you go, I need you to give us a sample." He raised a hand to reveal the test tube and the cotton swab contained inside it.

Rachel frowned and reached for it as he walked to the table and held it out to her. "DNA sample?"

"It's standard procedure," Travers lied, causing her to share a silent look with Tuck. They both knew something must have happened to warrant asking for the sample, but Celida wasn't about to say it in front of Rachel even if the woman had probably already figured it out. "Just rub that on the inside of your cheek for a few seconds and put it back in the tube."

Rachel took it and turned away to collect the sample, all ladylike. When she turned back with a questioning look on her face, Travers gestured for her to come around the table. "Let's drop that off to someone at the lab on our way downstairs."

He waited until she was out the door before shutting it slightly and addressing Celida and Tuck. "Either of you know where Evers is?"

"Still at work, I assume," Tuck answered.

Travers focused on him. "Get him here ASAP. Just in case."

"Just in case what?" Celida asked, already thinking the worst. But if they'd found a body, why not tell them? If new evidence about Rachel's brother had come in, she was entitled to know, and she wanted to be prepared so she could break it to Rachel gently. Travers had about as much tact as a sledgehammer.

Travers shook his head. "Don't know for sure yet. Just get him here," he repeated, and walked out of the room to follow after Rachel.

****

Poised in a single file line outside the concrete

building, Jake's team waited in absolute silence as the minutes ticked past.

Stealthy, efficiently delivered violence were the key to a successful op. The kind where everyone went home in one piece, hopefully after either acquiring or neutralizing the target.

The solid hand on Jake's left shoulder tightened a moment before the command came through the team's earpieces. The helmet-mounted night vision goggles revealed a landscape of almost neon green in what would otherwise be pitch blackness.

"Execute."

At the signal the team's breacher, two men ahead of him in line, rammed the locking mechanism on the steel door and blew it wide open. Their point man threw in a flashbang before the door had even hit the wall. A second later a loud bang and a blinding flash of light lit up the darkened room as the team surged forward as one unit.

"FBI! Everybody down!"

Jake raised his MP5 that they used for close quarter battle and put the stock to his shoulder. Moving in a choreographed rush that only came from countless hours of training together, the team entered the building.

Immediately Jake focused on the people in the room. Four tangos—two on the floor holding automatic weapons, one by the back door looking like he was going to make a run for it, and the last holding a male hostage with a pistol to his head. They'd already known how many hostage takers would be in here from the intel briefing. Now it was just a matter of clearing the room and getting the hostage out safely.

In the lead, Bauer took out the guy by the back door with a double tap to his center mass. The man behind him took one of the tangos on the floor while Jake and another teammate fired at the man holding the hostage.

Two rounds hit him in the head. Two more shots rang out almost simultaneously, signaling the end of the last man on the floor.

It was all over in less than ten seconds.

Jake and another teammate swept the room as one ran to the hostage and the others stood guard. He moved to the dead tango by the back door and kicked the rifle from his hands. There were no tripwires, no booby traps that Jake could see. No wires on the windowsills, walls, floor or the back door.

Turning his back to the door, he hurried over to where his teammate had verified that the other hostage takers were dead. "Clear," Jake called out.

"Clear," his teammate confirmed.

Bauer covered the distance to the hostage in two long strides and hunkered down beside the team medic. "What's his status?"

"Conscious and alert. Minor injuries. We're good to go."

Without another word Bauer slung his rifle and hoisted the hostage over one broad shoulder. "Let's go."

Jake took up position behind him and watched the back door carefully in case other tangos they didn't know about might be waiting outside. The team exited the building and ran to the mobile command post.

Agent DeLuca, a former HRT member now in his mid-forties, pushed a button on his phone and spoke. "One minute forty-two seconds from time of entry. You ladies are getting' slow in your old age."

"Slow my ass," Bauer grumbled, dumping the 150 pound dummy off his shoulder so it hit the ground with a thud.

"Shoulda been in and out of there in a minute and a half, tops," DeLuca continued as though Bauer hadn't spoken.

Jake and the rest of the guys took the criticism in

stride. DeLuca knew his shit and only wanted the best for and from them. The op had been a total success: no one on the team had been injured, the hostage was safe—well, kinda, since "he" was currently laying in a tangled heap on the asphalt of the warehouse parking lot here at Quantico—and all four tangos were dead.

DeLuca stood and stretched his arms over his graying head, giving them all a smile. "All right, you bastards, you're done for the day. Do your debriefing, then hit the showers and get outta here. I've gotta home-cooked Italian feast to go home to tonight."

They'd made note of things the team needed to improve upon next time, taking nearly an hour to wrap everything up. After showering and changing into fresh clothes, Jake pulled out his phone to check for messages, already looking forward to seeing Rachel again. There were four texts, two from Agent Morales and two from Tuck. It was the second one of Tuck's that sent a ribbon of unease through him.

Something's going down. Get up here ASAP.

Frowning, he called Tuck's number. "What's up?" he asked when his roommate answered.

"They took a DNA swab from Rachel earlier, told her it was just procedure. Travers wouldn't tell Morales and me what was going on but he's asked Rachel to stay here and I think he's waiting for you to show up before he spills it."

Oh, shit, that couldn't be good. "Any word on her brother?"

"No, but I'm betting they've got new evidence and Travers is just waiting for the DNA test to confirm."

Christ, he didn't want to think about her having to identify Brandon's body later if that's why they'd taken the sample from her. "I'm leaving now. Tell her I'm on my way."

"No offense, but that's just gonna worry her more.

I'm not gonna even tell her I talked to you but I'll stay with her until you get here."

Jake knew his buddy had somewhere else important he needed to be right now, so he appreciated the gesture even more. "Okay. Thanks, man."

"Forget it. I'll just add it to—"

"To my tab," Jake finished, already planning to make it up to Tuck by switching a shift so he could have a day off as soon as possible to see his dad. "Yeah, you do that. See you in a few." He jumped in his truck and drove as fast as he could through the remainder of rush hour traffic to the Baltimore field office. Morales was waiting for him at the front door with an uncharacteristic worried look on her face.

"She knew something bad had happened," she said as he fell in step with her through the lobby to the elevator, her quick strides conveying her urgency. "She insisted Travers tell her what was going on and wouldn't take no for an answer when Tuck and I tried to stop her, so he just took her down to the lab a few minutes ago."

"Ah, hell." And dammit, he wished Travers had sent her back to the hotel in the meantime rather than make her sit here all night, confirming her suspicion that something was wrong. "Is her brother dead?"

She shook her head. "I haven't heard that they located him yet, so it can't be that."

Then what the hell did they need to match DNA samples to? When the elevator doors opened Jake hurried down the hall to the lab. Tuck was waiting outside the glass door and headed over when he saw them.

"Sorry, man, I couldn't change her mind about coming down here."

Jake's jaw clenched, concerned only for Rachel and what she was being told right now. "Did you tell Travers I was on my way?"

"Yeah, and I gave him your ETA, too, but when we tried to stall Rachel she wasn't having any of that. She's no dummy, man."

No, not even close.

Jake didn't respond, just headed for the door that would let him into the lab. A flash of movement in the window caught his attention and he slowed when he saw Rachel standing next to an exam table, in profile to him as Travers spoke to her. Inside the room, a door at the back opened and a lab tech wearing a white lab coat came out carrying a plastic evidence bag.

Jake stopped as Travers barked something at the man. He couldn't hear what was said but his brows lowered menacingly and the tech quickly jerked the bag behind his back as he scrambled back to the door he'd just come out of.

Too late.

Rachel's hands flew to her mouth and she reeled back a step, her entire face draining of color. Even through the thick glass he heard her cry of horror and it sliced at his insides.

"Fuck," Jake snarled, and lunged for the door handle. He wrenched it open, ignoring Travers and the lab tech. Rachel's head swung around and her gaze locked on him, her eyes liquid with unshed tears.

She dropped her hands from her mouth and her face crumpled. "Jake," she choked out, immediately turning and lunging for him.

He caught her and held her to his chest, locking his arms around her back. She was fucking *shaking*, every muscle vibrating with a tension so great he expected her to snap.

What the fuck? He met Travers's angry gaze, didn't understand what the hell was going on until he looked down at the evidence bag the lab tech held...

And saw the human finger inside it.

Chapter Nine

Rachel buried her face in Jake's chest and squeezed her eyes shut, her whole body shuddering in revulsion. His arms were tight around her, one hand sliding up to cup the back of her head as he turned slightly, like he was trying to either shield her or block her view.

It was too late to shield her, and she never wanted to see that hideous sight again anyway.

The image of the severed finger was permanently seared into her brain. Knowing it was Brandon's was...

She sucked in a breath, swallowed repeatedly as her stomach rolled and her mouth flooded with saliva. God, she couldn't even think of what her brother had been forced to endure without wanting to puke.

This was her fault. She'd agreed to do the drop with the altered plans, and this was Xang's payback. Mutilating her innocent brother to send a clear message to them all.

And it was possible he'd done much, much worse, and sent this little piece of Brandon to taunt her.

Jake brought her even closer, his hold shifting so that he was cradling her. "Okay. Okay, honey, breathe."

She fought back the nausea, forced the grisly image

from her mind and focused on drawing in a painful breath.

"What the hell were you thinking?" Jake barked over his shoulder, she assumed at Agent Travers.

"She wasn't supposed to see it, it was goddamn shitty timing," he answered, and from the emphasis on the last word she knew he was chastising the lab tech. Sure enough, the scrambling of feet followed his words and the door at the back clicked shut.

Jake wasn't done. "Why the hell would you let her in here? You knew I was en route—"

"Jake." She curled her fingers into his T-shirt, holding on with the last of her control. "Get me out of here." Her voice wobbled and she was desperate to get some privacy before she broke down completely in front of everyone.

She'd fought to make Travers bring her down here with the very line that haunted her now. *Don't you dare treat me like I'm some weak female because you're afraid I'm going to fall apart. If you know something about my brother, you damn well better tell me right now!*

Now she was on the verge of doing just that and she couldn't stop it.

"Okay, babe. Come on." Keeping her tucked tight against him, he maneuvered her out of the lab and into the hall. "Give us a few minutes," Jake said to someone.

"Take her in here," she heard Morales answer.

Rachel didn't lift her head, didn't want to face anyone or have anyone see her like this except for Jake. He walked her sideways down the hall and another door opened.

"Tuck and I'll make sure you guys have some privacy," Morales continued.

"Thanks," Jake said, and closed the door behind them.

Finally alone without any prying eyes to witness her breakdown, Rachel stopped fighting the inevitable. A low, painful moan tore out of her gut. The tremors in her muscles turned to full-on quivering, so strong they hurt. She choked back a sob, the pressure in her chest unbearable.

"He's t-torturing him," she managed, fisting Jake's shirt now.

"Ah, hell, baby…" He pressed his face against her hair and just held her while the torrent tore through her.

She appreciated that he didn't try to quiet her or give her false words of reassurance. Jake was her anchor in this storm of fear and devastation and she was so grateful to have him there. The pressure of his arms never let up while the shock ran its course. Tears were beyond her at the moment, trapped too deep beneath the weight of the horror pressing down on her.

Rachel leaned into him, letting him support her as she struggled to get her breathing and heart rate back under control. With one deep, shaky breath she finally released his shirt and lifted her head, quickly turning away to wipe at her damp face. Jake eased his hold but kept a hand against the middle of her back.

"Want to sit down?" he asked her.

"No." Her voice sounded raw and scratchy, as though she'd been crying for a long time when in reality she'd been doing everything possible not to. She needed Jake to see that she was strong, that she could handle this, because she needed to see this through. One way or another, she was getting her brother back.

She cleared her throat, smoothed her hands over her own shirt to avoid looking at him. "I want to know how they got…that," she said, unable to say finger without wanting to throw up, "and whether or not he's still alive."

"Let me find out all that. You sit here and I'll—"

"No." She said it with such force that Jake's head jerked back a little. "I want to hear it straight, without any of you filtering it."

He studied her for a long moment, then sighed and nodded. "All right. But as soon as we're done I'm taking you back to the hotel. You're not staying here a second longer than necessary. Got it?"

As long as she found out whether Brandon was still alive or not, she'd leave. "Fine."

"Come on, then." He slid an arm around her waist and opened the door. The feel of that solid arm supporting her gave her strength. Her legs were a bit unsteady but she kept pace with him, studiously avoiding looking at the lab door as they passed it. Tuck and Celida were waiting a discreet distance away. "We're going to see Travers," he told them.

"We'll come with you," Tuck said, and hit the elevator call button. They rode in silence up to the floor where Travers's office was located, finding him at his desk talking on the phone.

He ended the call when he saw them and spoke to Rachel. "You doing okay?"

She nodded, thinking that was the stupidest damn question he could have asked her. Jake stayed right next to her, his hold at once protective and possessive. There was no doubt in her mind that she loved this man. "How did you get it?" She didn't need to clarify what she meant.

"It was delivered in a sealed packing envelope a couple hours ago."

"By mail?" Jake pressed.

Travers shook his head. "Hand-delivered."

"By whom?" Celida demanded. "You get them on video?"

"Third party. This time Xang used an old woman to make the delivery." He turned the monitor of his computer around and used the mouse to start a clip of the video feed. An old woman of Asian heritage carried a padded envelope up to the door, stood there for a second in uncertainty, and seeing that the office was officially closed, left it leaning against the door before walking away.

Travers stopped the video. "There was a note with it. It's down in the lab undergoing further analysis, but it's hand-written in Mandarin. One of our agents translated it as saying 'This is your doing, daughter of Li-Jiao'."

Cold flashed through her. "That's my mother's Chinese name. Brandon must have told him." It proved that her brother had been alive at the time the note was written, at least.

"Fingerprints on the envelope aren't Xang's, but the ones on the…evidence are," he finished, glancing at Rachel with an almost apologetic look in his eyes.

She swallowed, suppressing another shudder of revulsion. "Is my brother still alive?" Jake's hold remained rock steady. Her heart was pounding again, every hope and prayer focused on that.

"We don't know, but it doesn't make sense to send us a piece of him if he wasn't, and forensics told us it was taken from him while he was alive. We're doing everything we can to track where the package originated from and we're still tracing his earlier texts to you."

But they had no solid leads for a location on Xang and had no idea where Brandon might be. "So it's likely he's still alive." She needed to hear it from him out loud.

Travers inclined his head. "Yes."

Rachel inhaled, let it out slowly, aware of a heavy wave of fatigue washing over her. "So what happens now?"

"You want me to be straight with you, right?"

"Yes." Hard as it was to hear the truth, she needed

to.

"We need a break or a good piece of intel to help us find Xang. Once we find him, we find your brother."

He didn't need to tell her it could take days, weeks, or even longer for that to happen. And that the longer it took, the less chance her brother had of surviving this nightmare. "What can I do in the meantime?"

Travers leaned back in his chair, his eyes gleaming with something close to respect as he watched her. "You can go try to get some sleep. We'll notify you if anything more comes in. Morales will check in with you, keep you updated while we work the investigation."

"I'll see if I can get some time off, but if not I'll be with you when I can," Jake said in a low voice, his arm tightening around her.

"I'll help out with anything you need too," Tuck said from behind her.

She glanced over her shoulder, gave him a little smile. "Thanks."

Jake's fingers flexed on her waist, reassuring, protective. "Anything else you want to know?"

"Can't think of anything right now." Now that her most urgent questions had been addressed, as much as possible anyhow, she was exhausted.

"Let's go." Jake turned her away from Travers and walked her out of the office. He spoke to Celida and Tuck on the way to the elevator. "I'm taking her back to the hotel now. I'm due in at HQ at oh-five-hundred with Bauer, and Tuck, I know you're in tomorrow as well. You'll check in with her in the morning?" he said to Celida.

"You don't even have to ask," she told him. "Either of you need anything tonight, let me know."

"Will do."

After saying goodnight he hustled her out to his truck and drove her back toward her hotel. "Cold?" he asked, eyeing the way she was huddled in the passenger seat. It hadn't escaped her notice that he kept checking all the mirrors as though he was watching for someone who might be following them. Made sense, and she was glad for his vigilance, but it didn't make her feel any safer to be reminded that she was still under threat as well.

"A bit." It was the memory of that severed finger that kept slamming into her brain. She couldn't stop imagining what that had been like—for Brandon to scream and plead while Xang sawed off his finger. Had he even tended Brandon's wound afterward? Her brother could have bled out from such an injury…

"Here." Jake placed his leather jacket over her. She dragged it up over her shoulders, the scents of leather and Jake helping to calm her racing thoughts. He angled the heat vents in the dash at her and turned the fan on high. Soon her body was warm enough but her feet and hands were still cold and clammy.

"When's the last time you ate?"

She thought about it. "Can't remember but the thought of food right now makes me want to throw up."

"We'll order you something later if you feel like it."

"Okay." They rode in silence for another ten minutes before he spoke again.

"I'm so damn sorry you had to see that, babe."

"Me too." Although she was far sorrier about what her brother must have endured. She fidgeted with the edge of the leather coat. "Do *you* think Brandon's alive?"

"Yeah."

She turned her head to look at him. "Do you think Xang will send in more pieces of him?"

He shifted in his seat, for the first time looking like he wanted to avoid the subject. "I don't know," he said finally, his tone full of regret. "But I do think he's doing this to get back at you. Either for rejecting him or because of what happened during the drop."

She appreciated his honesty. "I'm not giving up on him," she announced as Jake took the turnoff to her hotel. "Maybe it sounds stupid in light of everything that's happened, but until I see Brandon's body for myself, I won't believe that he's gone."

"I understand. I'd feel the same way," he said quietly. "And he needs you to keep believing he'll be okay."

Nodding, she looked back through the windshield, silently acknowledging that her hope was fading with each passing hour. But if Brandon could endure what he had—might still be enduring, she thought with another shudder—then she owed it to him to hold on too.

****

Pumped from the recon mission he'd just completed, Xang slipped down the darkened alley and let himself into the side door of the warehouse. The heavy metal door groaned open, exposing nothing but blackness inside.

Pulling his weapon out of his waistband, he stepped inside and eased the door shut behind him.

Silence greeted him and for a moment he wondered if his prisoner had bled to death while he'd been gone, despite the rudimentary bandaging. But when he walked deeper into the cavernous room he at last made out the sound of shallow, raspy breathing.

Xang smiled. "Ah, so you're still with me," he said to Brandon, a barely discernible lump on the mattress in the corner.

He strode over and used the small pen light on his keychain to illuminate the area. Brandon lay on his side, his mangled right hand cradled in his left where he was still applying pressure to try and slow the bleeding from the amputation. The gauze bandage Xang had found in a first aid kit and hastily wrapped around the stump of the finger, was saturated with blood. Brandon's face was shiny with sweat, his skin grayish in the beam of light.

"I just saw your sister," Xang taunted, enjoying the anguish in the younger man's eyes. "She saw what I did to you." He'd broken into a building on the opposite corner from the FBI office and set up on the third floor, using a set of binoculars with non-reflective lenses to watch who came and went. He'd been in position when the old woman had dropped the envelope off, had watched when someone had brought it inside.

And he'd been there not only to watch that same dark-haired man in the pickup from earlier arrive, but also to see him walking out of the building with Rachel. He'd made sure to stay far enough back to avoid detection, then had the cab he'd called for follow the pickup to the hotel.

The irony of it made him chuckle. "I know where she's staying." Now it was just a matter of finding out what room she was in. He assumed she was smart enough not to be listed there under her own name. Once he found out the room number though, it would be simple enough. Provided the men he sent after her could take care of her FBI guard dogs.

Xang knew just who to send from his network.

He had the whole thing planned out already, and he would act on his own, without the cell leaders knowing. They weren't here, weren't on the ground and wouldn't be directly involved with planting the bombs. The beautiful thing was, he didn't even have to be involved with the rest of it. All he had to do was get in touch with some of the maintenance people he knew the cell already had in place. If they could successfully pose as maintenance workers, then it shouldn't be too hard for them to pose as housekeeping for a few hours.

They could get Rachel before executing the main attack, he could kill her himself and then he'd have proven his worth to the men financing everything from back in China. They'd have irrefutable evidence that he was much more than just a talented hacker.

Smiling to himself, he leaned forward to peer into Brandon's wide, terrified eyes. They were glazed with pain…and dread. "I've got plans for your sister," he said softly. "But first, maybe I should send her another souvenir." He reached down for his knife, drawing it slowly from the sheath, savoring the blank terror in the other man's eyes as he held up the blade so it gleamed in the light.

Brandon shrank away, shaking his head frantically, a ragged sob muffled by the filthy gag stuffed into his mouth.

Laughing, Xang straightened but kept the blade where it was, letting him anticipate more torture. Unfortunately he'd lost too much blood now for Xang to risk another amputation so quickly. Killing Brandon now wouldn't be any fun at all.

Chapter Ten

After checking with hotel security and the handful of agents around the perimeter to ensure there had been no suspicious activity throughout the day, Jake accompanied Rachel up to her room. As a precaution he made her wait outside while he swept it, then let her in and closed the door behind them.

She'd refused to eat, not even room service, and though she'd kept a brave face on the trip from the office, she wasn't sure how much longer she could keep control of her emotions. Part of her wanted to be alone to lick her wounds in private, and the other part didn't want Jake to leave yet. She was afraid that once she was alone that she'd crack in half and never be the same again.

Jake stood at the door, rubbing a hand over the back of his neck as he watched her shrug out of his coat and drape it across the chair with the ottoman. "Sure I can't grab you something?"

"I'm sure. Have you eaten though?"

"I'm good."

While she was grateful for his presence, she was also mentally and emotionally drained. "It's pretty late and I know you must have had a long day, plus you've got to be up early again for work tomorrow. I'm okay now if you want to go." She knew there would be someone posted at the hotel to provide extra security for her, maybe even Celida.

His hand dropped from the back of his neck and his expression changed. Hardened even though the intense glint in his eyes told her he wasn't angry. "There's no way you're 'okay'," he fired back.

At the moment all she felt was numb, but she didn't know how long that would last. As much as she wanted Jake to stay she didn't want to appear needy or clingy, even if she had good reason to be. She already felt fragile enough right now, the last thing she needed was to make herself completely vulnerable to him, and she would if he stayed.

There was no way she could be alone in this room with him for any sustained amount of time and not reach for him, or let her feelings for him show again as they had earlier during that kiss. She had no idea if he wanted a long-term relationship and she couldn't do any other kind with him.

"I'll be fine," she said quietly, lowering her gaze to where her hands were folded in her lap. He saw her as calm and serene. She liked that image far better than the chaos inside her right now, and didn't want to embarrass herself by letting him see it. "I'm going to have to call my mom. I can't put this off any longer."

"What are you going to tell her?"

"The basics, at first. That he's been kidnapped and that the FBI is handling it." Not very well, in her opinion, but it would hopefully comfort her mother to know an investigation was already underway.

"You're wiped. Call her in the morning."

Rachel sighed. "I couldn't sleep. Not now. Every time I think about how scared he must have been when—" She stopped, swallowing back the lump in her throat, waited until the tightness lessened before continuing. "As soon as I close my eyes, that's all I'm going to see."

Jake came away from the door in a surge of movement. Rachel stiffened and leaned back, instinctively retreating from him and that hard look on his face. But he merely stopped a foot from her, dropped down and reached out to slide a hand around her nape.

His palm was warm against her skin, his long fingers flexing gently against the tight muscles. She forced herself to meet his gaze, shock ripping through her at the raw intensity she saw there.

He shook his head once, a muscle working in the side of his thickly-stubbled jaw. "I told you once I'd do anything for you. Do you remember?"

Mouth too dry to form a response, she nodded.

His fingers squeezed, the increased pressure still gentle but conveying his sincerity. His urgency. "I meant it."

Swallowing, she found her voice. "I know."

Those dark eyes never wavered from hers. "Then say what you need. Ask me."

"Ask you what?" she whispered, suddenly feeling emotionally naked.

"Ask me to stay."

She desperately wanted that, but only if it's what he wanted. Because they both knew he'd stay if she asked. Just like they both knew what would happen if he did. Once they crossed that invisible barrier, everything would change. Things had already been so emotionally intense over the past two days. Was she ready to make that leap after just finding him again? Was he?

He gave her a tiny shake, impatient. "Babe. *Ask* me." He was so fierce, so determined to comfort and support her. It melted all her resistance.

Taking a deep breath, forcing aside the scary feeling of vulnerability, Rachel reached up to grip his hard forearm. She made herself hold his gaze as she answered, her whisper barely carrying through the space between them. "Stay."

****

The moment she said it Jake let out a relieved breath and lowered his hand from her neck.

She was staring up at him with a mixture of hope and longing that made him ache. Her trust, her willingness to let him in when she needed him most were more precious to him than any gift he'd ever received. He knew how hard it was for her to lean on people—from the first time he'd met her he'd seen how much she cherished her independence—so the fact that she wanted him to stay enough to ask was huge.

Christ he wanted nothing more than to scoop her up, strip her naked and crawl between the sheets with her, bury himself as deep as he could get in her warmth and give her something good to concentrate on for the next few hours. Because he knew damn well she wasn't ready for that at the moment, he forced himself to take a step back.

"Go take a long, hot shower and relax." Whatever happened between them tonight, he didn't want her to be nervous or have regrets later. Even if he just got to hold her all night long, he was good with that. He'd have left if she'd asked him to, but it would have killed him to walk away from her tonight.

Rachel nodded and got up to disappear into the bathroom. While the water ran, giving him images of what her naked body would look like gleaming wet beneath the spray, he went ahead and ordered some room service. The food had just arrived twenty minutes later when the bathroom door opened, releasing a cloud of steam.

A second later Rachel appeared in the threshold, wearing a long-sleeved sleep shirt that came to mid-thigh. His gaze zeroed in on her breasts, which she quickly covered with her arms, then down to her long, bare legs. Knowing she was naked beneath that shirt made every muscle in his body go rigid with longing. Her clean vanilla scent hit him from the other side of the room, making him hungry for a hell of a lot more than food.

Still in the doorway, she lowered one arm from her chest and tugged self-consciously at the hem of her sleep shirt. "There was no robe," she said, looking first at him and then past him at the food.

Ah, honey. "Come and eat," he said, his voice gruffer than he'd intended.

She shook her head and opened her mouth but he didn't give her a chance to argue. She started to take a step back but he got up and caught her hand, tugging her back over to the chair with him.

Before she could protest he hooked an arm around her waist and pulled her into his lap, sinking back into the upholstery. She was stiff against him, tugging at the hem that had ridden higher up her thighs, but at least she didn't pull away. Jake pulled in a deep breath, savoring her sweet scent.

"I'm still not really hungry," she murmured, avoiding eye contact.

"I just want you to eat a few bites," he said, and selected a piece of cheddar cheese from the tray. Lifting it to her mouth, he held it there and finally she relented, taking his wrist and parting her lips.

He pulled his hand back, waited until her eyes flashed up to his before shaking his head once, then put the cube at her lips. Fascinated, he watched while the blood rushed to her cheeks, staining them a rosy pink.

Her lips parted and she took the morsel from his

fingertips. She might not have meant it to be a sensual gesture, but with her innate elegance and femininity, it was. He went rock hard in his jeans, the weight of her pert little ass nestled there an enjoyable form of torture.

Neither of them spoke as he continued to feed her little tidbits from the tray. Grapes. Berries. More cheese. After her fifth mouthful she pushed his hand away and curled into him, resting her head in the hollow of his shoulder. Jake's heart squeezed.

He wrapped both arms around her and cuddled her close, nuzzling the damp waves of hair beneath his nose. She felt so damn good and he was grateful once again that she was turning to him for comfort. There was no way she could miss the feel of his erection pressing against her but Jake ignored it, focusing instead on the rapid beat of her heart beneath his palm at her back and the way she curled so trustingly against him.

It was more than he'd ever expected to have, and yet it wasn't nearly enough. He was aware of every subtle thing, from the sound of her breathing to the curve of her breast pressed against him and the way the damp strands of her hair caught in his stubble.

They stayed that way for so long that he was starting to wonder whether she'd fallen asleep, but then she shifted and rubbed her cheek against his chest. The action was feline and sensual and the press of her ass against his swollen cock made the need inside him flare to life.

Rachel turned her face up to his, those pretty hazel eyes searching his for a moment before she curled her hand around his nape and put her mouth on his. The kiss was slow and soft, everything the last one wasn't. Jake let her set the pace, willing to give her whatever she needed right now.

He ran his palm up and down her spine, moved lower to map the curve of her waist and hip before gliding up to her shoulder. Rachel murmured in pleasure and deepened the kiss, dipping her tongue into his mouth. Jake followed her lead as their tongues played, building the heat until she was squirming in his lap and her nipples were hard little points outlined by the thin material of her shirt.

Without breaking the kiss she reached for his hand and lifted it to cup one of her breasts. She moaned into his mouth when he squeezed the soft flesh and rubbed his thumb over the straining tip, arching her back for more.

Jake took over. He trailed a damp line of kisses across her jaw and down the side of her neck, finding the places that made her shiver and twitch as he played with her breast, his scruff leaving little red marks on her delicate skin. He wanted to see those marks all over her body later, a sign of his possession. Her breathing increased, the throb of her pulse accelerated beneath his caressing tongue.

Keeping her distracted with the kisses, he reached down to fist the hem of the shirt and slowly begin to pull it upward. He felt her throat move beneath his mouth as she swallowed, but her hands curled deeper into his shoulders and she lifted her hips slightly to allow him room to move.

Inch by inch he eased the soft material upward, revealing more and more pale gold-toned skin. He caught just a glimpse of the neatly trimmed triangle of hair between her thighs before he drew the shirt up over her abdomen, up her rib cage to her breasts.

Fisting the wad of material against her sternum, he lifted his head to gaze at the pert flesh he'd revealed, topped with pale brown nipples. They were beaded tight, a fine scattering of goosebumps covering her silken skin.

Unable to stop himself, he slid the hand at her hip upward until it rested between her shoulder blades and dipped his head to taste her. The instant his lips touched her she gasped, her muscles tensing. He placed teasing, reverent kisses over the velvety curve, then let his tongue play with the stiffened center, rubbed his bristly cheek against her tender skin. She hissed in a breath and grabbed the back of his head, holding him close.

Jake didn't need encouragement. He took her into his mouth and slowly sucked, rolling her nipple against the roof of his mouth. Rachel moaned and squirmed in his arms, growing restless.

He took turns pleasuring each breast, letting his hand slowly trail down the center of her body to the apex of her thighs. His fingertips brushed light patterns against her inner thighs, coaxing her to open for him. She did, slowly, making the victory all the sweeter. And when he slid his fingers across the slick, swollen flesh between her legs, they both moaned.

The feel of her wetness made his erection throb painfully and the heady scent of her arousal made his heart hammer. He wanted in her so bad he could barely see straight, but tonight was all about her and what she needed.

Gliding his fingers through the wet folds, he feathered over the taut bud at the top of her sex, drinking in her soft cry. He eased one finger into her, then a second, pumping gently before withdrawing to stroke her clit again. Within minutes she was trembling, her breaths choppy. Her fingers bit deep into his shoulders, her eyes glazed as she stared into his and moved her hips in time with his hand.

She buried her face into his neck. "Jake, I need more."

Instantly he stopped. Withdrawing his fingers from inside her, he ignored her whimper of protest, holding her tight around the hips as he got to his feet and walked the short distance over to the bed. With one hand he jerked the coverlet down and set her on the edge of the bed, pulling her hips so that they rested on the very edge.

As he sank to his knees in front of her, her legs snapped together and she curled an arm over her breasts. Still holding her hips prisoner, Jake looked up to find her blushing and biting her lip.

A smile tugged at his mouth. "You're not seriously feeling shy with me now, are you?"

She lowered her gaze. "It's just...this is really intimate."

Oh, shit, the thought of getting his mouth on her, of sliding his tongue inside her and listening to the sounds she'd make had him hard all over. "Yeah. And I've been wanting to go down on you forever."

Her gaze snapped to his. "Y-you have?"

It surprised him that she seemed shocked by that. He bent to place an open-mouthed kiss on the top of her left knee. "Mmhmm. I wanna taste you so bad, babe, you have no idea. So just lie back and relax for me." He wanted her to come against his tongue so badly his heart was pounding.

She gulped and slowly lowered her arm from her chest, revealing the softy rounded breast he'd tasted just a minute ago. "I just—whoa." Her arms jerked out to the side, fingers curling into the sheet as he bent and kissed the top of her mound.

He smiled at her reaction. With careful pressure on the inside of each knee he gently pulled her legs apart. She let him, lying back and watching him as she bit her lower lip once more, still shy, a little hesitant. Feeling the lingering tension in her body, the uncertainty in her, Jake suppressed a primal growl at the sight of those tender, flushed folds revealed to his gaze.

Lowering his head he kissed her sensitive flesh, absorbing the jolt that shot through her body. Kissing and nibbling his way down, he flattened his tongue and gave her a long, slow lick that ended in a tender swirl around her clit. Rachel gave a soft cry and released the bedding to plunge her hands into his hair.

Hell yeah. Jake closed his eyes to better savor the feel and taste of her. Soft, teasing licks over the super-sensitive bud at the top of her sex, then the firm thrust of his tongue as he drove it inside her. Over and over he alternated between the two, finding out what pressure and rhythm she liked best. Soon she was moving restlessly beneath him, her hips lifting into his mouth, unable to hide her need.

"Jake, please."

God, he loved hearing that breathless plea from her. Much as he'd love to draw this out for a long while yet, he didn't want to torture her. This was their first time together and he was going to make sure he kept the trust she'd placed in him.

Holding her hip in a dominating grip that commanded her to stay still, he pushed his fingers into her as he flicked at her swollen clit. Rachel mewled in pleasure and arched her lower back, pressing her pelvis against his tongue.

That's right, babe, just enjoy what I'm doing to you.

She was so damn sexy and he was so freaking hard, but all the torment was worth it to see her come undone beneath his mouth. Curving his fingers, he found the sweet spot behind her pubic bone, rubbing with a firm pressure while he laved her sensitive bud. Her throaty moan filled the room and he could feel her inner muscles squeezing his fingers, the telltale flutters alerting him that she was getting close.

He kept the pace steady, not wanting to rush her, wanting her to enjoy every second of this. Her hips rocked against his mouth, her inner walls tightening, tightening…

A whimper escaped her, changing into a series of

ecstatic cries as she dug her hands in his hair and shattered. Jake kept stroking her until the last pulses faded and she collapsed back against the sheet, breathing hard. Withdrawing his hand, he kissed her thighs and abdomen before getting to his feet and shifting her up toward the headboard.

Rachel murmured something unintelligible and went willingly, eyes closed. Immensely pleased with himself, trying like hell to ignore the brutal throb between his legs, he pulled the covers over her before settling in beside her. His head had just hit the pillow when she rolled and cuddled into him, draping a leg across his thighs and an arm across his chest.

Her hand smoothed over his chest. "What about you?" she murmured drowsily.

"I've got everything I need right here," he murmured back, hugging her close. "Get some sleep." This wasn't some game or contest to him and he sure as hell wasn't keeping score. He didn't want her thinking she owed him because of what he'd just done.

More importantly, he wanted to show her that he would put her needs before his own whenever he could. All the shit he'd gone through in Afghanistan and Pakistan with the Titanium crew had made him realize just how much she meant to him. Tonight she needed to be taken care of, whether she wanted to admit it or not.

He stroked her hair, enjoying the silky texture of it as it slid through his fingers. Her contented sigh washed over him, the languor in her body telling him just how tired she was and just how satisfying that orgasm had been.

With her cheek resting in the hollow of his shoulder and her weight nestled so perfectly against him, Jake reached over and turned off the light, already dreading having to leave her.

Chapter Eleven

Xang jerked awake, his foot slipping off the edge of the bed frame. He shot upright, reflexively raising his pistol and aiming toward the door. His pulse thudded in his ears as he strained to make out the sound that had woken him.

Faint light from the streetlamps outside streamed through the dirty windows set into the top of the warehouse walls. He didn't hear any footsteps outside, no voices, just the occasional coo of a pigeon that had made themselves at home in here.

Lowering his weapon, he glanced at Brandon. He was splayed out on his back, his cuffed left hand still clutching the bandage on his right even in sleep. The pressure dressing had pretty much stopped the bleeding during the night so the gauze was now dry and a rusty color. His face was still pale, with shadows beneath his eyes.

It was a sight to break any sister's heart, and from what he'd heard from Brandon, Rachel was more sensitive and loving than most. That was going to work to his advantage.

He got up and walked to the corner to take a piss against the concrete wall. As he was finishing up, the burner phone in his pocket buzzed. He zipped up before pulling the phone out and checked the display out of habit, though he already knew it had to be his someone from his network.

For two seconds he thought about ignoring it, then decided he'd better find out what whoever it was wanted. "Yeah," he answered warily. Whatever they wanted, it had to be urgent if they were calling at this hour.

"I heard a rumor that you're planning an operation of your own."

Xang scowled at the sound of his contact's voice, ignoring the chill that shot up his spine. The gang member he'd thought was so loyal had freaking tattled on him like a grade schooler and given out his number? Really? "Maybe I am." He didn't give a shit what they thought anymore. If they had his number they could have tracked him if they'd really wanted to, and killed him already. So they must still need him.

But if he decided to cooperate, it was happening on his terms. He was taking charge of his own destiny to use to his advantage later. The bigger the bargaining chip he came to the table with later, the better. Adding kidnapping and the murder of Rachel and Brandon to his résumé was just the start.

If the cell leaders didn't have him killed first for operating on his own.

"This could be to our advantage," his contact added.

Xang paused, already seeing where the man was going with this. And how Xang could benefit from it. "Go on."

"Word is that the FBI is getting close to learning what our target is. Taking the woman hostage at the right time will help divert their attention at the critical moment."

And he could demand a lot more money from them

afterward. "I've already worked out the details."

"So change them. We're willing to lend you our men and our firepower. But you have to work with our schedule."

His eyes cut to Brandon, still asleep on the filthy mattress. He could stomach working with their schedule—if it benefitted him. "What's in it for me?" Chances were they'd just kill him once they got Brandon. He had to make sure they'd still need him afterward, otherwise he'd be stupid to consider this plan.

A low laugh. "Pull this off correctly, and you get to live. A well-paid, comfortable life as long as you remain useful to us. Much better alternative than living on the run, staying in abandoned warehouses, don't you think?"

Anger punched through him, but it was rapidly extinguished by a cold wave of fear. He knew by the edge buried in that taunt that they had his location. Probably had eyes and ears on him right now that he wasn't even aware of.

Xang cast a furtive glance around, wondering if that's what had woken him earlier. He knew what the cell did to people who failed to carry out orders. He'd rather die by a quick shot to the head from an assassin than suffer for days on end with what these men did to their enemies. Things that made what he'd done to Brandon look civilized.

He wiped at the sweat gathering on his upper lip. Now it was imperative for him to ensure that he would still serve a purpose after this op. "When do you want this done?"

"This afternoon."

Xang wanted to laugh, but the man just kept on going. "One of my men will be in touch with you within the hour. He'll come get you and give you everything you need. Make sure you bring the brother with you, for collateral."

"Fine," he said grudgingly, knowing he had no other choice. Besides, the money was the most important thing. With enough cash he could disappear, start over somewhere else where they would never find him and carry on the war his way.

His contact ended the call. Xang pulled out a penlight, stalked over to the mattress and nudged Brandon none too gently in the ribs with the toe of his boot. The man awoke in a rush, his face contorting with pain and fear the moment his squinting eyes locked on Xang.

"Get up," Xang said, reaching for the cuff he'd locked to the bed frame. "We're leaving. Got a hot date with your sister I can't afford to miss."

****

Jake woke when Rachel stirred in her sleep. He lifted his head to check the bedside clock and saw it was just after two in the morning. He carefully rolled to his side and lowered his head onto his pillow, the digital display of the clock giving just enough illumination for him to see Rachel. She was on her back with the covers tangled around her legs. She'd slept off and on for the past couple hours but she'd been restless, unable to slide into the deep, restful sleep she needed.

Her legs twitched again and she woke. She seemed to start in the darkness, the sound of her indrawn breath loud. "Jake?" she whispered, turning her head to look for him.

"Right here." He slid a hand around the back of her shoulder and she rolled into him, draping her arm across his chest and her bare thigh over his with a sigh of relief that tugged at his heart. He turned onto his back to wrap his arms around her, nuzzling the top of her head and breathing in the clean scent of her hair. "Can't sleep?"

She shook her head, her cheek rubbing against his T-shirt. "I'm so tired though."

He made a sympathetic sound and began sifting his fingers through her hair. It was soft and silky and the touch seemed to relax her. "Don't force it. If you can't sleep, just rest." She exhaled and snuggled into his body, setting off the inevitable reaction of making him harden against her belly. Ignoring it, he continued to stroke her hair while he ran the fingertips of his other hand up and down her bare back. This was all so hard on her and would continue to take its toll until they got Brandon back safely and arrested Xang.

They lay like that in the darkness for a while, Rachel warm and relaxed in his embrace. Her unchanged breathing rate and the alertness in her body told him she was still awake. Then her fingertips began rubbing over his left shoulder blade in a soothing motion. "What did you do during those years we were apart?" she finally asked softly.

The question surprised him. "Worked. Trained. Traveled."

"I mostly worked too. Didn't travel much except a couple trips to China to see my mom," she said. A long pause spread between them before she continued. "I tried to get over you but never could."

His hand paused on her back, fingers stilling in her hair, but she continued before he could say anything.

"I really missed you," she said.

God. He'd never imagined she'd still been waiting for him. "I missed you too, babe."

She was quiet a long moment. "Why didn't you ever tell me that you broke up with Linda? You never did in all the time I wrote to you. Not even this last time when you e-mailed me six months ago."

"The truth?" He sighed. "Right after we broke up I wanted to tell you. I thought about it a lot, about you, but

I knew if I told you then chances were good we'd wind up together and it wouldn't have been good. My training schedule was insane, I was gone more than ever, and I wasn't in the right headspace to be in another relationship."

He resumed playing with her hair, reading the lack of tension in her body. She didn't seem mad or hurt by his explanation so far, which relieved him. "Then I worked on that NSA taskforce on a long-term op and when I was overseas the last time some really bad shit went down and I realized what a complete and fucking idiot I was for keeping you at arm's length. When I got back I looked you up as soon as I could and you made it pretty clear you'd moved on—which I deserved—so I wanted to respect your wishes and didn't say anything because I didn't think it would make a difference."

"I lied," she murmured, her breath warm through his cotton T-shirt. "I kept trying to move on, but I compared every guy I dated to you and they never measured up. And then I started wondering if I was just building you up in my mind, spinning unrealistic dreams about you and what it would be like if there ever *was* an us. It was killing me to pretend I was okay with just being your friend and keep hoping for more, so I made up my mind to sever contact and move on whether I wanted to or not."

Yeah, he'd screwed all that up pretty bad. He was damn lucky she'd reached out to him again. He hated that she and her brother were in this kind of danger now but without it they might never have seen each other again. "I should have told you." He should have been up front about what was going on and let her decide whether she was still willing to be in a relationship with him at that point.

She nuzzled her cheek against his pec, stirring a shower of sparks under his skin. "Yes, you should have.

But at least we have now."

He kissed the top of her head, something about her words making him uneasy. "You don't mean *just* now though, right?"

"No, not for me, but where do you want things to go from here?" Her body was still, a subtle tension invading all her muscles. It floored him that she might be worried he was only looking for a fling. He made a vow to show her just how much she meant to him.

"I want to do this right. Make up for the mistakes I made back then." Jake slowly ran his palm down the length of her spine, back up again.

She huffed out a soft laugh. "That's not really an answer. What do you want now, with us?"

He smiled in the darkness. "Okay. I want *you*. Only you. For as long as you'll have me."

The residual tension bled out of her muscles. "Careful, 'cuz that might be for a very long time," she warned playfully, trying but failing to smother a yawn.

"I'm up for it." He was up for something else right now too, but he knew how exhausted she was and that reality would intrude again in just a few short hours. Shifting onto his side, he gently turned her over to face away from him and tucked his bent knees behind hers, wrapped an arm around her ribs and slid the other beneath her head. She settled into him with a sleepy, contented smile.

"You never did get around to taking me to the range," she murmured. "I still want to learn to shoot. We can tape a picture of Xang's face to the targets. That should help my aim even if I've never fired a weapon before." Her tone held a hard, wry edge.

Sounded downright therapeutic to him. "I'll teach you anything you want to learn." She'd be a quick learner, and motivated. She'd always been interested in what he did, the skills he'd acquired in his line of work.

It'd be fun to teach her.

"Rappelling too?"

The thought of her sweet ass hanging directly above him, framed by a climbing harness as he literally taught her the ropes… Not exactly a hardship. He smiled in the darkness. "Sure."

She relaxed even more. "Thanks."

"Think you can sleep now?" he whispered, pressing soft kisses to the nape of her neck. He wouldn't be able to, not with his cock pulsing the way it was, pressed so tight to her ass. But holding her like this while she slept, with Rachel relaxed and trusting him to take care of her was a gift he was going to savor.

"Mmm, think so."

She was fast asleep within minutes, the sound of her breathing slow and even. A wave of protective tenderness washed over him. He lay awake in the darkness for a long time before following her.

****

Rachel's eyes fluttered open in almost complete darkness and it took a second to remember where she was. When she did her heart immediately did a little flip and she rolled onto her side expecting to find Jake, but the other side of the queen-size bed was empty.

She jerked her head off the pillow to look toward the door as disappointment swamped her, then realized she could hear the shower running in the bathroom. Laying her head back on the pillow for a moment, she considered her course of action. Twice during the night she'd woken fresh from the grip of a nightmare about Brandon, and Jake had been there to take the sharpest part of the fear away. He'd been incredibly tender and generous with her last night, taking care of her needs while ignoring his own.

And now he was naked in the shower just steps away.

She knew he'd be leaving soon and that she'd be facing whatever happened today without him. Rachel didn't want to let him go without the chance to explore that hard body the way she'd always dreamed of and give him some pleasure in return.

Pushing aside the shyness that had gripped her last night, she got out of bed and ran her hands through her hair on her way to the bathroom. Normally when she was in a new relationship it took her a long time to get comfortable being naked in front of her new lover, but Jake was unlike any man she'd ever been with. He'd been her friend first, was standing by her through this whole nightmare and she wasn't going to let a little nervousness stand in her way.

The cracked-open bathroom door gave way when she pushed on it. Instantly her eyes shot to the shower. Jake stood under the spray, his broad, muscular back to her behind the glass as he tipped his head back to wet his hair. Just the sight of him like that, knowing she was about to kiss and caress that powerful body, made her a little lightheaded.

She pushed the nagging guilt about her brother aside. There was nothing she could do to help Brandon right now. Jake's job was dangerous—something could happen to him today. These last few minutes before reality crashed back in were for her and Jake alone.

Grabbing the travel bottle of mouthwash from the sink that Celida had thoughtfully packed for her, she took a quick swill and rinsed out her mouth. Overcoming shyness was one thing; morning breath the first time she ever got to enjoy Jake was quite another.

She pulled open the shower door, still a little shocked at her boldness. But she kind of liked this new Rachel who went after what she wanted.

Jake half-turned, a welcoming smile spreading across his face as she stepped into the enclosure with him and shut the door. "Morning." His dark gaze raked over the length of her naked body, triggering an instant rush of heat beneath her skin.

"Morning," she murmured, drinking in the sight of all those gleaming, wet muscles and the dark hair on his chest, the narrow line of it that bisected his defined abs and trailed out of view. His ass and powerful thighs were gorgeous too.

"Sleep okay?"

"Mmm, yes." Before she could lose her nerve, she wrapped her arms around him from behind and pressed up tight against his back, resting her cheek between his water-slick shoulder blades. She flattened her palms against the sculpted planes of his chest, savoring his heat and the crisp texture of the hair on his chest, heart thudding at the feel of all that masculine power beneath her fingertips. She trailed them gently over his wet skin as she lifted up to kiss his nape, then trail a damp path down to the center of his back.

Jake set his hands over hers and squeezed once, leaning back into her body in a clear signal for her to continue. She did, gladly, allowing herself to explore him with her touch, the warm rush of water cascading over them acting as a kind of cocoon.

Her fingers trailed across his pecs and down the hard, flat ridges of his abdomen, pausing when she brushed against the head of his erection standing proud against his belly. She rubbed her breasts against his back, soothing the ache in her tight nipples, and slid her hand lower to curl around his hard flesh. He was thick and hot in her grip and the half growl-half groan that came out of him made her sex instantly wet.

Jake turned to face her, letting her hand stay curled around him. She couldn't help but steal a peek at his erection, all dark and swollen with need, then looked up into his eyes for a split second before he gripped a handful of her hair and tugged her up to meet his kiss. It was deep, wild, hungry. He tasted of mint toothpaste and she was once again glad for the mouthwash as she rubbed her tongue against his.

Rachel sighed into his mouth and began stroking both hands up and down the length of his cock, varying the pressure to see what he liked best. His hips rolled, thrusting into her touch while that hand in her hair held her in place for his kiss.

But she had other ideas.

Tugging against his hold, he released her and she trailed a string of kisses across his jaw, her teeth scraping over stubble as her mouth moved down his neck to his chest. She let her tongue play there, tasting the spicy flavor of his skin as she flicked it over his hard nipples and earning an indrawn breath from him before working her way down and sank as gracefully as she could to her knees. Jake slid one hand back into her hair and when she glanced up the length of his body into his face, his eyes had gone molten with desire.

"God, you don't know how beautiful and sexy you are like this," he said in a gravelly voice, fingers flexing in her hair, exerting just enough pressure to pull deliciously against the wet strands.

She wanted to drive him crazy, make him lose his mind with the pleasure she bestowed. Smiling up at him, she held his gaze as she leaned forward to kiss the tip of his erection, her tongue stealing out to lick the flared head. He hissed in a breath and tensed, all his muscles standing out in sharp relief, his other hand shooting out to brace himself against the slick fiberglass wall. She'd never felt so sexual, so completely feminine as she did then, on her knees preparing to go down on this incredibly powerful man.

Parting her lips, she took the thick crown inside her mouth and sucked. A low, rumbling groan came from his throat, his fingers squeezing in her hair, then caressing her scalp in an almost drugging motion. He tasted salty, tangy. Hot and wild. Her tongue licked around the sensitive head. She let her eyes drift halfway closed and lost herself in giving him as much pleasure as she could, taking him deeper.

"Baby, ahh…" His hips rolled slightly before he stopped himself, and she felt the slight tremor in his muscles. Holding back as though he was afraid of hurting or scaring her, yet desperate for more.

She was going to give him exactly what he needed.

Rachel set her other hand against his upper thigh to brace herself and felt the way the muscles quivered and tensed each time she sucked and swirled her tongue around him. She loved knowing she could affect him so much.

The hand in her hair tightened when she sucked harder, fingers clenching tight. "Sweetheart, you're gonna make me come."

She murmured in encouragement and kept going, hungry for the taste of him, to please him, ignoring how her own body pulsed with desire.

"Rachel." His voice was strained, guttural, and it stroked over her tingling nerve endings like a caressing hand. The fingers in her hair tightened, pulled her head back so that she had to release him. She eased back on her heels and stared up at him, licking her swollen, sensitive lips. His stare was hot enough to burn, his nostrils flaring with each ragged intake of air. "Does sucking me off make you hot?"

She nodded, heart pounding, not wanting to risk breaking the spell by speaking. Sucking him had made her so wet, she was all slick and ready for him. *Needing* him.

Jake's nostrils flared as he inhaled and reached for her, those big hands curving beneath her arms to haul her to her feet, biceps and triceps bulging. She gasped as he turned them and pressed her back against the slick wall, his big body pinning her there, the wild, unsatisfied hunger vibrating between them. Her hands gripped his slick shoulders.

One hand cupped her jaw to tilt her mouth up for his kiss, his tongue sliding along hers while his other hand gripped her left thigh and lifted it, opening her sex to the hot length of his erection. She shuddered in his masterful hold, her breasts and sex throbbing. He kissed her hard and deep then flexed his hips, rubbing the length of his cock against her slick folds, the tip caressing her swollen clit. Her needy whimper sliced through the rush of the water, her whole body stiffening under the sudden lash of intense pleasure.

With a low, hungry sound in reply, Jake brought her leg even higher so she could wrap it around his hip and give him better access to her body. She was dizzy, drowning in bliss but she needed so much more. Squirming, she rubbed against him in turn, adding to the friction, the incredible heat. *Not enough. Not nearly enough.* "Ah, God, Jake…" She slid one hand into his hair, gripped tight.

He reached a hand between them to grip the base of his cock and position the swollen head against her opening. Then he paused. "I'm clean," he grated out.

"Me too," she managed, barely able to think, just wanting him inside her, stroking all the throbbing, aching nerve endings he'd awakened.

"You on the pill?"

"No," she moaned in distress, digging her fingers into his hair, his hard shoulder and tightening her thigh around his hip so he wouldn't retreat. She didn't think she could take it if he did. Maybe it was reckless and stupid to continue without protection but in that moment she didn't care about the consequences as long as she got to feel him inside her.

"I'll pull out," he muttered against her mouth, nipping her lower lip before sliding his tongue across it just as he flexed his hips and the crown of his cock pushed inside her. Rachel caught her breath and squeezed her eyes shut at the hot, heavy penetration, pulling her mouth free to press her face into the curve of his shoulder. He was only in her an inch or two but he was so damn thick and the delicious stretch, the friction, felt incredible. All she could do was moan and roll her hips in a silent plea for more, her open mouth sliding against his wet, heated skin.

With a rough growl Jake eased out of her and did it again, stopping partway in, that slow, shallow slide of rigid flesh rubbing over the hot glow inside her. His hips pulsed, sliding him in and out over and over while he slipped a hand between them to rub his thumb around her clit in slow circles.

Ohhh... Rachel trembled, her inner walls tightening around him, squeezing that glorious thickness inside her. "Don't stop," she gasped out.

"Hold on." A command and a warning.

Rachel held on, eyes squeezed shut, her entire body trembling. His thrusts grew deeper, more forceful, his mouth working the side of her neck, short beard prickling her while that hot tongue dragged over sensitive nerve endings. Heat and pressure built inside her, robbing her of thought, the ability to breathe.

She distantly heard the plaintive moan that tore from her, knew she was holding his shoulders so tight she was probably leaving marks but couldn't ease up. The pleasure, this slow, relentless climb he was forcing her to make instead of racing to the summit, was tearing her apart.

Helpless in its grip, she writhed in his unbreakable hold and let it expand until it broke over her. It felt like she was dying. Jake's mouth smothered her wild cries as the orgasm took her, adding his own deep groan of male satisfaction. The waves were still breaking when he drove deep once, twice, then wrenched out of her body.

"God," he moaned, his head tipping back, eyes closed and a tortured expression on his face. He was the most beautiful thing she'd ever seen, and *she'd* done that. Made him feel so good the pleasure bordered on pain. Triumph shot through her, blending with the residual waves of orgasm.

Jake let out a ragged groan and leaned his weight on the arm braced against the wall, his muscles cording. His fingers dug into her hip to hold her still and a deep, hoarse cry spilled free as he fisted himself and started to come across her belly in hot spurts.

Breathing hard, he bent his head to bury his face in her neck and just held her while they came back to themselves and the hot water rushed over them. Rachel lowered her foot to the shower floor and let him hold her up, her legs weak and shaky.

"You don't know how many fucking times I fantasized about that," he murmured.

She smiled against his hair. "Was it worth the wait?"

"*Hell* yeah." He nuzzled the side of her neck and slid his hands over her wet skin, making her shiver with longing. "What about you?"

It turned her heart over that he might be worried about not meeting her expectations. She kissed his hair in reassurance. "Yes. So, *so* good."

He hummed in satisfaction. "And just so you know, there are a lot of other things I've thought about doing to you. Really *hot* things."

"Have you?" she teased.

"Yes, ma'am."

"What are they?" She wanted to know every secret, dirty thing he'd ever wanted to do to her. She had plenty she wanted to do with him.

"You'll just have to find out." His left hand smoothed over the right cheek of her bottom then delved between her thighs to stroke between her legs. A primal rumble came from deep in his chest when he felt how wet he'd made her. "My naughty, gorgeous girl." He sounded extremely smug and pleased about that.

Rachel closed her eyes and wriggled in his hold. "It's already after four," she said, regretting that they didn't have more time together.

His hand stilled and he scowled. "Hell."

Yes. "But maybe you can show me some of the 'things' you have in mind later on."

A hard finger slipped beneath her chin and tipped her face up until she met his eyes. "Babe, that's a promise."

A shiver zipped through her. Grinning, he picked up the bar of soap and quickly washed himself off while she helped, getting distracted by all the muscles on display. "You feel amazing," she murmured, awed by the sheer masculine power of him. "Is it okay if you're a bit late today? I don't know if I can stop touching you."

A choked laugh sounded from above her and he caught her wrist when she slid a soapy hand down to wash between his legs. He was still partially hard and she wondered if she could make him ready for her again right now. "You're not helping the situation," he admonished with a grin, "but I'm glad my body turns you on. That'll just motivate me more next time I hit the weights." He turned slightly to rinse off.

When he got out she stayed to have her own fast shower and was just wrapping a towel around her body when he came back into the bathroom dressed to leave.

"Morales texted me, said she'll come by around seven-thirty or so."

"Okay, but she doesn't actually have to hang out with me in the room if she doesn't want to." She knew how busy the team was trying to find Xang and Brandon.

He snorted. "Babe, she's coming up whether you want her to or not, so get used to the idea."

That dark, heated gaze swept over the length of her body from face to toes and back, leaving a trail of heat that licked across her skin, then he settled both hands on her hips and tugged her close. "Make sure you take care of yourself today. Eat a full meal for me. I'll be back as soon as I can." He pressed a slow, lingering kiss to her lips before raising his head. "Anything comes up, just text me and I'll get back to you when I get it."

"Okay. Be careful out there and have a good day."

He grinned wider. "Thanks, *dear.*"

She was smiling when he walked out the door a minute later. They hadn't talked at all about what was happening between them or what their expectations were going forward, but she knew what she felt was real. That what they had together was real. It wasn't casual and she was certain he felt the same way.

But now that he'd left, reality crashed back in, turning her thoughts back to Brandon. For now she had to keep hoping that the FBI would find her brother. Once that happened, they could all move on with their lives. And not until.

Chapter Twelve

L owering herself into the upholstered chair set off to the side of the hotel room, Celida eyed Rachel. The woman looked like she was in desperate need of some coffee. She knew Jake had stayed the night with her but whatever had happened between them was none of Celida's business so she didn't ask. "So. How are you holding up?"

"As well as can be expected, I guess." Rachel took the other chair opposite the occasional table. "Any news you can share on the investigation?"

After Brandon's finger had been delivered, the FBI taskforce had basically pulled an all-nighter. "We've narrowed down the list of targets. A few of the hotels are hosting important conferences in the next week or so, and one is where a few upper level Chinese officials are supposedly staying. Since the terror cell Xang is connected to is part of a separatist movement and they've targeted Chinese interests in the past, we think they want to hit something here owned by the Chinese government. To make a statement, yada yada."

That story got fucking old real fast when it got repeated ad nauseum throughout the world of radical Islam. "We've got teams going out this morning to check each location."

Rachel nodded. "What about Brandon?"

There was no easy way to say it. "Sorry, nothing."

Blowing out a breath, Rachel nodded and looked down at the carpet. "But he could survive that kind of injury, right? I mean, with all the bleeding and stuff."

"Yes. And if Xang went to all this trouble, the thinking is that he wants your brother alive so right now we assume he must have given him some kind of medical treatment to keep him that way." Rachel was smart—Celida didn't have to point out that anything could have happened between the time of the amputation and now.

Rachel tipped her head back to rest against the chair. "I had to call and tell my mom this morning."

"How'd she take it?"

"Not well. He's her only son. Even though my dad was an American and we were raised here, she's still traditional Chinese in many ways. Brandon is her only son, so…"

So he was the center of her world. "But you and your mom have a good relationship?"

"Oh yeah, I know she loves me to death. She was a good mom and never treated me any different than him once he came along. It's just—I know how close she is to him. He'll always be her baby. When my dad died six years ago she moved back to China to be with her family and took Brandon with her while I stayed here and finished my schooling. I didn't want to move over there so he came back here when he started college." She shifted in her chair, met Celida's gaze. "Are you close with your parents?"

Celida hated talking about her personal life and her family, but she liked Rachel and knew she wasn't trying to be nosy. "I lived with my mom up until she died. My dad remarried about ten years ago and I don't see him much." Only when she had to, actually.

"I'm sorry about your mom. Your dad must be proud of you though, going through the military and then into the FBI. Just like Jake did."

She shrugged. "Maybe. But I don't care what he thinks, to be honest." And that was enough about that topic. "So what's the scoop with you and Jake?" She hoped they'd at least moved beyond the friend zone after all this.

A light pink stained Rachel's cheeks and she shifted in her chair again, clearly uncomfortable. "Um…"

Trying not to laugh, Celida waved a hand to stop her. "It's okay, I get it, and I wasn't looking for the gory details." She couldn't help but smile. "I'm glad. Jake's a good guy."

"He is," Rachel answered with a grin.

Okay, maybe she wasn't done with this subject quite yet. Her natural curiosity was what made her a good investigator, and it was pretty damn clear how Rachel felt about him. "How long have you been in love with him?"

Rachel went dead still, her eyes shooting to Celida's. "What? I mean, I'm not…"

"You are too. Come on, I'm not gonna say anything to him. Just curious." And clearly it had been way too long since she'd been out with her girlfriends if she was this eager to know about this.

Rachel cleared her throat, looked away as she answered. "I can't put a date on it. But I've had…really strong feelings for him the past couple years."

Really strong feelings? Yeah, she could relate to that too. And love maybe wasn't the right term for what she felt for Tuck anyhow. Half the time she wanted to rip the man's clothes off and do very bad things to him, but the other half he made her want to strangle him into unconsciousness. "Cool. I hope it all works out for you guys. I think you're good for him."

A shy smile curved her lips. "Thank you. I hope so."

Okay, girl talk over with.

Celida stood, tugging on the hem of her charcoal gray pencil skirt that went awesome with her lipstick red pumps. The skirt was snug around her hips and ass with a flirty little bow at the top of the seam just beneath her cheeks, but stretchy enough that she could still move comfortably. And if Tuck should happen to show up at some point today and just *happen* to get an eyeful of her...*assets*...so much the better.

"We might be called to one of the buildings to assist if the team wants to check anything about the blueprints with you," she said to Rachel.

"That's fine. I'm ready whenever, and I kind of hope they do call me in because I'm already getting a serious case of cabin fever."

"Understandable." She checked her watch. "Let's give them a half hour to—" She broke off at the sharp knock on the door.

"Room service," a slightly muffled male voice called out.

Celida looked at Rachel. "You order breakfast?"

She shook her head, looking surprised. "No. Think Jake might have?"

"Doubt it." Though she supposed he could be pulling out all the stops to show Rachel his romantic side.

With a hand tucked into the side of her blazer, Celida grasped the grip of her sidearm. She took a cautious step toward the door. "I didn't order room service," she called out. And she distinctly remembered seeing the Do Not Disturb sign on the door handle when she'd come down the hallway.

"I've got breakfast here for a Miss Granger."

She could text Jake to check, but she knew he wouldn't be near his phone right now, and he would have told her if he'd planned to pull this kind of surprise. This didn't feel right. "No thanks."

"We have to deliver it, ma'am."

We?

Glancing behind her at Rachel, she murmured, "Stay there." Withdrawing her service weapon, she silently crept to the door and snuck a peak through the peephole.

Sure enough, two uniformed men stood next to a cart with a tray covered by a silver dome. Last time she checked, it didn't take two men to deliver breakfast for one.

Instincts on alert, she looked over her shoulder at Rachel and waved her toward the bathroom with an urgent motion of her hand. Rachel's eyes widened but she got up and hurried to the bathroom. The moment she started moving, Celida turned her attention back to the door, already backing away.

With her free hand she reached up and tapped her earpiece. "This is Morales," she whispered. "Two suspicious men outside principal's room—"

Three silenced shots ripped through the door, splintering the wood. A searing pain hit her left forearm as another round grazed her cheek.

She fell back against the wall and slid to the floor, but still managed to get off two shots through the door. "Rachel, lock the door!" she shouted, right hand shaking slightly as she aimed at the door and returned fire again.

Her third shot had just punched through the wood when the door burst open. She threw up an arm to deflect it but wasn't fast enough. The edge of it slammed into the side of her head. Black spots swam in front of her vision.

"Morales, you copy?"

She couldn't respond to the male voice coming through her earpiece.

"Morales!"

The attackers were already inside. Backup was down in the lobby, they'd never get here in time.

Fighting through the pain and disorientation, she managed to raise her weapon. A boot smashed into her right wrist. She cried out in agony, lost her grip on the Glock. A wave of dread crashed over her. If they got past her, Rachel had no chance.

She forced a shaking hand up to shield her face, failed to block the foot that kicked her in the side of the head and turned her world black.

****

Oh shit, oh shit...

Rachel scrambled to lock the bathroom door and crawled into the bathtub as the gunshots rang out from inside the room. Heart in her throat, she huddled there uncertainly.

There was no way out other than the way she'd just come in, and she didn't know how to help Celida. Her phone was back on the bedside table.

The return fire stopped and the front door crashed open, then an ominous silence filled the room. Celida must be down.

No!

She frantically looked around her to find some kind of weapon—anything to defend herself with. Her gaze landed on a can of hairspray.

She lunged over to grab it, held it poised in front of her with her finger on the nozzle. It wasn't much but when they came through the door she might be able to temporarily blind them and give her a few seconds to get out of the room.

Quick footsteps sounded in the other room, coming closer. She pressed back against the tiled wall. Trapped, with nowhere else to go.

A sickening burst of fear exploded inside her when a foot slammed into the lock. Once. Two times as she cringed and prayed that backup would arrive in time.

On the third kick the door splintered around the door handle and it flew open to reveal two Asian men wearing hotel uniforms. The first one stopped in the doorway, a chilling smile forming when his gaze lit on Rachel cowering in the tub.

"You gonna shoot me with that?" he taunted in Mandarin, his laugh skating down her spine with icy fingers.

She flung out her arm and shot the smug bastard right in the face with the hairspray. He howled and wiped his eyes. Rachel shot to her feet, prepared to jump out of the tub and make a run for it, but the second man was there, blocking the doorway. She froze, heart hammering against her ribs.

The first man stopped scrubbing at his face and shot a bone-chilling glare at her. She was too terrified to scream, hoped that the shots had alerted someone on the floor to what was unfolding here.

He raised his pistol like he was going to hit her with it but the other guy grabbed him by the arm to stop him. A battle of wills ensued for a few seconds and she noticed the second man was bleeding from a wound in his left shoulder. Celida had shot him.

Good.

The first man jerked out of his hold, his red, runny eyes shooting sparks at Rachel. He lunged forward and knocked the can out of her hand with an angry swipe. The sound of the metal clattering on the tile floor was loud in the terrible silence.

Without a word he seized her by the upper arm and

dragged her from the tub, easily overpowering her resistance.

"Let me go!" she shouted, yanking and twisting with all her might. All it got her was a burning sensation as her skin twisted in his steely grip. "Let me go!" she screamed again, this time in Mandarin.

The man jerked her so hard her head snapped back and she landed on the floor on her knees before him. Before she could move he wrenched her arm behind her and seized a handful of her hair, still holding his weapon, and glared down at her with an oily smile that told her exactly what he'd like to do to her in this position. Rachel glared up at him in defiance, terrified but determined to fight him to the last.

The second one reached past him to grab her by the upper arm and haul her to her feet. Without pause he started dragging her toward the hotel room door and she caught her first sight of Celida, lying face down on the floor. Dark puddles of blood were pooling around her and Rachel couldn't see where she'd been shot but Celida was moaning and moving slightly.

The man holding her aimed his weapon at the agent and Rachel reacted without thinking. She shot a hand up and grabbed his wrist with an outraged, "No!"

He met her eyes for a second, but relented when the sound of voices came from the other end of the hall. Cursing, he yanked her up against him, his grip bruising as he jammed the muzzle of his pistol under her chin. The cold metal bit into her skin and she started shaking.

"You come with us without any trouble or I shoot you," he threatened, and Rachel knew he would do it without a second thought. He shook her once, hard enough to make her teeth clack together, then shoved the weapon against her lower back. "One shot to the kidney and you'll bleed out while you beg me to kill you just to make the pain stop."

It scared her to death, but why go to these lengths to kidnap her if they wanted to kill her here and now? They could easily have shot her in the tub already. He had to be bluffing. And better to die here and now by a gunshot or be wounded as she ran, rather than let them take her and do God only knew what later.

She opened her mouth to scream, had just gotten the first blast of sound out of her restricted throat when one of them wrestled something wide and sticky across her mouth. Duct tape.

She bucked against the iron hold restraining her and threw her head back, hoping to ram the one holding her in the face, but the back of her skull bounced off his chest. She kept screaming and struggling but her cries for help were muffled, maybe too quiet for anyone to overhear. Which was what they'd no doubt intended.

Her stomach clenched, the fear threatening to close her throat off as she desperately dragged air through her nose. She kept fighting, doing her damnedest to gouge and claw and kick as she was dragged into the hallway.

Someone had to have heard those shots and her screams. Hotel security had to be on the way up, and the police would have been alerted. She just had to hold out until backup arrived.

The second man closed her room's door—maybe to block anyone from noticing Celida initially—and followed a few steps behind. A door behind them opened but whoever it was quickly snapped it shut again when the second man swung around and raised his weapon at them. Her legs felt like rubber and she didn't even remember moving; the guy holding her practically carried her down the hallway and into the stairwell, her struggles barely even slowing him down.

The whole time her mind was spinning, scrambling to come up with a way out of this. But they were too strong. Despite her every effort she was dragged along like a piece of driftwood caught in the surf.

At the bottom floor they exited out at street level into the bright sunlight. She squinted at the sudden glare. A dark car came around the corner and sped toward them. Its tires screeched as it came to a quick stop. The back door flew open and the man holding her shoved her headlong into the backseat.

She caught herself on her forearms, scrambled into a sitting position just as the other door flew open and one of her captors slid in. The second slid in on her other side and slammed the door shut, trapping her between them.

The car's tires let out a high-pitched squeal as the driver took off. She pushed her hair out of her face and angrily shoved against the men caging her as one of them tore the tape away from her mouth. It felt like her skin came away with it. "What the hell do you want with me?" she demanded, her voice hoarse, shaky.

"You're going to be our diversion, Rachel."

Her blood turned to ice at the sound of that familiar voice.

She watched in horror as the man in the front passenger seat turned to look back at her.

Xang.

Her skin prickled and the fine hairs at the nape of her neck stood up. "Where's my brother, you bastard?" she snarled.

"You'll see soon enough. He's dying to reunite with you." He smiled and held up a phone, showing her a picture of Brandon.

Her brother was bound to a chair, chin resting on his chest in a defeated posture that broke her heart, his mangled hand covered by a blood-soaked bandage. The image had been taken from an angle to the side and slightly from above. It took her a second to realize it wasn't a picture, but a video. She had no way of knowing if it was a live feed or not.

"Too bad it won't be a happy reunion," Xang finished with a smirk.

Turning to face front again, he tucked the phone back into his coat pocket while the car sped toward whatever fate he had planned for her and her brother.

Chapter Thirteen

A rmed with a tray full of pastries and specialty coffees—including a dolce cinnamon latte for Morales, because it was her favorite—Tuck approached the front entrance of the hotel and frowned at all the cop cars and emergency vehicles parked out front. When he'd texted Jake earlier to tell him he was on his way here, his friend had texted back asking Tuck to grab something for the girls to eat. But the sight that greeted him in the lobby had his internal alarm blaring.

Around a dozen cops were stopping people from getting on the elevators and questioning people coming out of the stairwells, so he knew something big must be going on and he was ninety-nine percent sure it must have something to do with Rachel. Then he noticed a group of men talking beside the elevators and his body stiffened when he saw Agent Travers there.

Shit, what the hell had happened? Tuck headed straight for him. The other men speaking to Travers fell silent as he neared.

"What's going on?" Tuck asked.

Travers clenched his jaw and shook his head once. "Two men stormed Rachel's room less than half an hour ago. They took her and shot Morales—"

"*What*?" When the man just stared at him in response, Tuck wanted to grab him and shake him. "Where is she?"

"We don't know, but the surveillance cameras show them taking Rachel—"

"Morales," he growled, his gut clenching at the thought of her being shot.

"She's still upstairs in Rachel's room. They're getting ready to transport her."

Tuck shoved the coffees and pastries at a guy standing to his left, didn't even wait to see if he caught them before racing for the staircase. The metal door clanged shut behind him as he raced up to the sixth floor, dodging people trailing down the stairs to the lobby. More cops were positioned by the door on the sixth floor but they let him through when he showed his badge.

He jogged the rest of the way down the hall, his heart stuttering when he saw the bullet holes in the door. Big ones, likely from .45 caliber slugs. They could kill from hydrostatic shock even without hitting anything vital. *Fuck.*

The first responders let him in after he showed his badge and he stopped dead when he saw Celida laid out on a stretcher, bloody bandages on her arm, face and head.

He strode right up to the side of the gurney, his gaze sweeping over the damage. Head and facial wounds bled a lot, so though she looked pretty bad, none of the wounds appeared to be life threatening. Her eyes were closed, a huge swollen knot forming above her right temple. Whatever they'd hit her with, that blow alone could have killed her.

God, sweetheart...

"Celida." He reached down to take her unbandaged left hand, wrapped his fingers around hers. Her pallor and stillness worried him. She was always so bold and full of sass, seeing her this way scared the shit out of him. Even though he knew the risks that came with her job he'd just never imagined her not being here, never allowed himself to think that something might happen to her. Had he lost her now, after being such a Boy Scout all this time by keeping things strictly professional between them?

"She's concussed," one of the EMTs told him as he finished hooking up an IV. "She's still pretty out of it."

Jesus, was there a skull fracture or something? He leaned over her, put a hand on the uninjured left side of her face. "Celida. Hey."

Her lashes fluttered and her eyes opened slightly. She blinked up at him, seemed to have trouble focusing but thankfully her pupils responded evenly. "They took her," she rasped out. "Didn't…stop them."

"Travers is already on it." He eyed the lump on the side of her head, the bloody bandage on her right cheek. "Damn, they marked you up pretty good, huh, sunshine?"

She blinked at him, whether because the endearment had just slipped out or she was having trouble concentrating, he wasn't sure. "Is it…bad?"

Likely they hadn't let her see her face yet, but the lack of a smart-ass remark told him just how worried and vulnerable she felt. She wasn't squeamish, but this was her blood they were talking about and he was glad she couldn't see it.

His muscles knotted with the need to scoop her up and hold her, tell her everything would be okay. But he didn't out of fear of hurting her more—because he knew damn well she'd never tell him if he did—and because he wasn't going to let his feelings flap out in the breeze for her and everyone else to see when he wasn't sure if she would push him away. Hell, he wasn't even sure if she was on the same page as him in terms of wanting a change in the status of their...relationship.

"Not that bad," he lied, though he'd certainly seen worse. "You're gonna have quite the shiner for a while though. How's your arm feel?"

"Not broken. Just sore. Flesh wound, I think. My wrist is worse." She sounded groggy as hell.

He gritted his teeth at the thought of those bastards shooting her through the door. He wished he'd been here. Maybe he could have made the difference in turning the tide of the attack, or preventing it entirely. Maybe Celida wouldn't have been wounded, Rachel would be safe and the suspects would both be dead.

Because, man, what he wouldn't give for five minutes alone in a room with those fuckers right now. He'd tear them apart, solely for what they'd done to Celida. Jake could have a turn on Rachel's behalf after that. Wherever she was, Tuck hoped she was okay.

Tamping down the primal rage burning through him, he kept his voice calm as he spoke. "You just rest and get better, okay? The team will handle this."

She started to nod, then winced as though the motion was agonizing. "Tell Rachel...I'm sorry." Her voice shook and a sharp pain lanced through him at seeing her so fragile and broken.

"Nothing to be sorry for," he argued. Hell, she'd taken at least two bullet grazes and by the looks of the way her eyes were already swollen half shut, nearly suffered a skull fracture trying to ward off the attackers. Celida was well trained and a deadly shot—he'd worked with her on the range personally many times to hone her skills—so if she'd been caught off guard and unable to take her attackers down, it could've happened to any of them.

He squeezed her hand once more, feeling helpless. During his years in SF and later in Delta it had always been hard to see a teammate wounded, but with her it was a thousand times worse. "Just rest and heal up. I'll be in touch but call me if you need anything. Okay?" he stressed, needing her to see that she could count on him. That he *wanted* her to.

The woman was notoriously independent and hated when anyone suggested she couldn't handle something on her own. He admired that to a point, but as a man he wanted the woman he was involved with to let him take care of her to at least some extent. Say, after getting shot and suffering a concussion, for example. Celida wouldn't see it that way, of course, which was one of the reasons he'd been wary of getting involved in a relationship with her. That pig-headed part of her personality drove him fucking nuts.

"Yeah." She closed her eyes as though the effort of speaking to him had completely drained her.

Reluctantly Tuck released her hand and stepped out of the way as the EMTs transported the stretcher out of the room. The forensics team would be in here shortly. And shit, he didn't know how the hell he was going to break this to Jake, assuming he could even reach his commanding officer to relay the message. But damn, he'd seen how Jake was with Rachel. In his shoes, Tuck would want to know immediately, and he'd rather hear it from a friend than from Travers or someone else.

He took out his phone and pulled up Jake's number but an incoming call interrupted him. When he saw his CO's number on the display, he silently cursed. "Tuck here," he answered.

"You need to get down here ASAP," the man said. "Your team's on standby for a developing situation."

"Has to do with a kidnapping?" he guessed.

"No. Bomb plot unfolding with mass hostages at risk. Get in here."

Shit. And he'd bet this also had to do with the cell that had Rachel.

He'd just have to try to reach Jake during the drive to Quantico. "On my way."

****

Jake's blood pressure plummeted as his commander's words registered.

Rachel had been taken hostage.

The kidnappers—Xang and some of his fellow cell members—had sent the FBI a link to a live feed of her and her brother, bound and gagged in an empty room on the top floor of a hotel she had helped design. The camera angle wasn't great, giving them only a limited line of sight into the room, but there was nothing they could do about the lack of visibility from here.

They'd have to go in blind because explosives had been planted in the building. One device had already gone off, starting a fire on the third floor. Fire crews were on scene with ladder trucks but they couldn't gain access to the building because of the threat of more bombs.

Recent chatter said that they were going to blow critical stress points in the building's infrastructure to bring it down like the Twin Towers, killing the nearly eight hundred occupants trapped in the floors above the fire if emergency crews didn't get them out quickly. Punishment for the Chinese government's harsh treatment of the Uyghur people, their economic ties to the U.S., and America's involvement in the War on Terror.

Seemed fishy as hell that all that chatter would just happen to be released as the plot was unfolding. The whole fucking thing stank of a setup and every man in the room thought the same thing.

Jake gripped the edge of the table so tight his knuckles turned white. It took a monumental effort to focus on the rest of the briefing. Team assignments. Threat assessment. Sniper positions. Primary and backup plans. Emergency exfil plans.

"Okay boys, let's do this thing right," DeLuca said, straightening. "Nobody goes in until the EOD teams give us the green light."

Jake didn't know if he could stand that—to wait on the sidelines for them to clear the building of explosives, all the while knowing they could go off at any moment and bring the building toppling down with Rachel inside it. The helos standing by at the airfield couldn't get them there fast enough for his liking.

DeLuca gripped his shoulder. "You tight?"

"Yeah," he forced out. All of his training, all his discipline meant shit in the face of the threat confronting Rachel. The only reason he was even still allowed on the op was because they couldn't afford to waste time trying to find someone to fill his spot. Every man on the team trusted him with their life, and vice versa. If he wasn't locked in, someone could die.

"Let's get loaded up."

In full tactical gear, they all headed to the vehicle pool. Other teams were already assembling to develop their own plans in case things went sideways and they needed multiple assault teams on site. No one knew for sure how many terrorists were at the hotel, if any. They might have planted everything then run like the fucking cowards they were.

Fighting like hell to stay in the zone and not think about Rachel's life hinging on the success of this op, Jake loaded into one of the trucks and the team raced to the airport where the helos were launched from. He jumped out with five of his teammates while two other vehicles unloaded in front of them.

Two sleek Blackhawk helicopters sat perched on the tarmac, rotors already turning. Once the order was given to launch, they could be on scene and infiltrating the hotel within eleven minutes.

But the waiting was goddamn killing him. Despite his effort to think only of the floor plans they'd studied and other critical info for the op, his mind kept jumping back to last night when he'd had Rachel naked and coming apart in his arms. Then this morning when she'd almost brought him to his knees in the shower, and the adoration he'd seen in her eyes.

He checked his watch for what felt like the dozenth time in as many minutes. Only seven had passed.

"Gotta give 'em time to do their job, man," Bauer rumbled beside him. "Until those bombs are found and taken care of, we're not going anywhere."

"I know." It just wasn't nearly fucking fast enough for his liking.

Tidbits of information began to trickle in as agents on scene updated them. One EOD team had found a device and was in the process of defusing it. The cops had already established a secure perimeter, and guests lucky enough to be escaping the hotel were being rushed away from the scene. The entire area was on lockdown.

God, he wanted to see that live feed again, just to assure himself that Rachel was still alive.

Bauer's big hand landed on his shoulder and squeezed tight. "We're gonna get her out, farmboy. Gonna pull this off like you read about."

Jake nodded, too keyed up to respond. To block everything out and get back into operational mode, he closed his eyes and focused on breathing. Envisioned the floor plan, how they were going to infiltrate the building, the turns they would make once inside.

A sense of calm began to spread through him, dispelling the fear and unease.

When he opened his eyes again, he was back in the game. All his teammates were there, locked and loaded, ready to go to work. And they were the best in the world at what they did, along with Delta and ST6. Some of the guys had come from those tier-one units.

"Wheels up in four minutes," DeLuca called out from the command truck, his phone held to his ear. "Radio and comms check now."

Jake's heart rate kicked up. Everyone checked that their communication equipment was working, then the team leader gave the signal and they all hustled for the helos, assault rifles at the ready. The pilots did their final check and the birds lifted off, climbing up to cruising altitude within a couple minutes.

Every man was quiet, each knowing their role, each knowing what was expected of him. When the hotel finally came into view, Jake's heart rate had steadied and there was a calm inside him that always overtook him during ops.

The Blackhawks circled the top of the building, and, seeing no visible threats, descended to hover just above the rooftop. The crew chief of Jake's helo readied the fastrope and gave a thumbs up to the team leader, who slid down to the roof. Jake was third in line. When it was his turn he gripped the rope between his gloved hands, clamped his boots together around it, and slid down.

Once on the ground he grasped his rifle and took a knee to provide perimeter security for the rest of the team who were still unloading from the birds. He knelt in position while the powerful rotor wash beat down on him, sending pieces of gravel and pigeon feathers scattering in the air.

A minute later the helos took off to return to base. At a solid thump on his shoulder to alert him the guys behind him were in place, Jake stacked up with the others at the steel door they were going to enter.

The team had been split into two assault elements;

one to breach the door, and Jake's to infiltrate the building first. Snipers were providing backup and giving them extra eyes on target. Someone from command would cut any remaining power to the building that hadn't already been damaged by the earlier blast the moment they breached the door. Once they found the room where the hostages were, Jake's team would enter and clear the room while the others provided security.

Two members checked the door for booby traps or tripwires, checked to see if was unlocked—it wasn't—and gave the all clear. The team leader gave the signal and the breacher slammed his breaching tool into the steel door. It swung open and the men poured through it, into the darkness lit up by the green glow of their NVGs.

"Clear!"

Now Jake's pulse picked up a notch. He followed close behind the man in front of him, sweeping past the other team down a short flight of concrete steps to an unlocked door. They checked for more tripwires and booby traps, then moved into the hallway beyond it.

A right turn into another empty hallway, then a left to another set of stairs. Down to the next level, another quick right turn and the room where Rachel was supposedly trapped lay on the left twenty yards ahead.

Silently the team made their way to the door. With no eyes inside and the snipers positioned on surrounding rooftops unable to see in here, they were all on their own. At a signal Schroder knelt down and used a snake camera to ease it under the door and take a sneak peak. Jake watched his teammate's every move and battled his frustration at being so close to Rachel and yet so far. Xang and his men might have wired the entire room—hell, the entire floor—to blow if they so much as jostled the door.

"Two hostages inside, no tangos," Schroder whispered, his voice barely carrying through Jake's earpiece. "I don't see anything rigged on the door."

Maybe Xang's crew had been more concerned with saving their own sorry asses and getting out as quickly as possible instead of wiring the place to blow.

The first man in line pulled out a universal keycard and waited for the order to try the door. They could blow it but it wasn't necessary and with no visible tangos around there was no need to use that kind of violent entry. Jake stayed in place as he awaited the team leader's signal to begin. He didn't allow himself to think of Rachel in there, instead focusing on what had to be done to protect his teammates, eliminate whatever threats were on the other side of that door, and then rescue the hostages.

Tense seconds ticked by. Fourteen. Fifteen. Nobody moved, staying absolutely still.

"Execute."

At the voice coming through their earpieces, the entry man slid in the keycard. A tiny green light appeared, signaling the door was unlocked. The entry man gingerly turned the door handle. When nothing exploded he pushed the door and the team poured into the room.

Through the green-lit display in his NVGs, Jake scanned the room. There were no tangos to be seen, just the two hostages strapped to their chairs.

Finally he allowed his gaze to focus on Rachel. She was tied to a chair, her back to him. She was looking over her shoulder right at him and the naked terror he saw in her eyes ricocheted through him like a hollow-point round. They'd gagged her, but she was trying to communicate to him, shaking her head so frantically that her hair rippled around her face. Even from where he stood he could see she was shaking.

And when she glanced pointedly back and down toward her bound hands then jerked her gaze back up to his, he understood it wasn't just because of her ordeal.

In her bound, trembling hands she was holding a live grenade.

Chapter Fourteen

If Rachel had been afraid before, now she was freaking terrified. Until now it had only been her life on the line if she released the pressure on the grenade's trigger or dropped it completely. Brandon was far enough away from her that the blast would hopefully only injure him.

But now Jake and his teammates were well within the blast radius. Her hands had long since gone numb—it was a miracle she was still even holding onto the grenade at all, especially when the team's entry had startled her. Her muscles jerked and trembled despite her efforts to stay still. Panic flashed through her.

Oh my God, please don't let me lose my grip!

Her whole body shook as she stared back at Jake. He couldn't have known how close he and his teammates had come to killing her when they'd entered, and maybe dying in the process.

After the initial shock of their entry, she'd picked him out right away despite the dimness. She knew the way he moved, the way he carried himself. He'd confirmed it when he'd stopped in his tracks to stare at her. Unable to speak or move anything but her head, she'd tried every way she knew how to warn him about the grenade.

Now Jake pushed up what looked like some kind of space-aged goggles on his helmet and started toward her. There was just enough dim light coming through the open door for her to see his face, his set expression telling her he was in full operational mode. She wanted to scream at him to stop, and yet she prayed he'd know how to get her out of this.

Stay still. You have to stay still. She sucked a shaky breath through her nose, prayed her finger didn't move off the trigger.

"Evers, hold up."

He halted, never taking his eyes off her hands. A man around the same height as Jake stepped forward and motioned for the others to fan out. "Check for tripwires."

Jake slung his rifle across his back and pulled off his gloves, still watching her. "You're gonna be fine, Rachel. Just stay real still and keep breathing for me."

At the sound of his voice something inside her simultaneously swelled and crumbled. Tears rushed to her eyes. She blinked to show she'd heard him, and a few tears slipped down her face.

The brave smile he gave her broke her heart. "Hang tight, we've got you. This will all be over in just a few minutes."

She kept her attention riveted to him as the team checked the room for hidden explosives. The man who she assumed was team leader called out. "Status."

"Clear," someone called from the other side of the room.

"Clear," Jake echoed from near her.

When all the team members responded the same, the team leader approached with Jake and a big man it took her a moment to recognize as Jake's friend Bauer. Bauer held up a small but powerful flashlight to give them light to work by while Jake and the team leader came to kneel behind her.

Jake stayed slightly to one side, allowing her to see him as they assessed the grenade. She was vaguely aware of others moving about the room and converging on her brother.

We're actually going to make it out of here alive. It was almost too much to take in after spending the last few hellish hours trapped here holding the device that so easily could have killed her.

Xang and his crew had dragged her up all those flights of stairs and by that time she'd been barely able to struggle she'd been so exhausted. They'd brought her in here, secured her to the chair so she sat facing her brother, who'd watched with wide, terrified eyes as one of the men had pulled the pin from the grenade and placed it in her hands. Xang had watched with a victorious smile.

"Hold the trigger," the leader said to Jake.

He did, wrapping one hand around her left wrist and squeezing gently. "I've got it, sweetheart. You can let go now."

She cast a glance down at him to be sure.

He met her gaze and nodded once. "I've got it," he repeated. "Trust me and let go."

Holding that trigger down had been the hardest thing she'd ever had to do, but letting it go was nearly as hard. Her numb fingers were frozen in a claw shape around the grenade. She could barely get the digits to respond to her mental command to relax.

Jake slipped the weapon from her grip while the team leader cut away the layers of duct tape binding it to her hands with what she assumed was a knife.

"See the pin anywhere?" the team leader asked.

"Nope," Jake answered. "But this was way too simple. I don't like the feel of it."

"No shit," the team leader grunted. "Call one of the

EOD boys up here to deal with this," he said to Bauer.

She heard Bauer talking to someone over the radio as the leader finished cutting the tape away. Her arms fell to the sides, limp and heavy. She winced and sucked in a breath as pain shot all the way up to the tops of her shoulders from having maintained the awkward position for so long.

"I'll take that," the team leader offered, and she watched as Jake carefully transferred the grenade to his teammate. "Go ahead and get that tape off her."

Jake knelt back down beside her and reached out to gently grasp the edge of the tape covering her mouth. He peeled it away slowly but it still stung like hell as it came away from her skin. A small whimper of relief escaped her when he pulled it all the way off.

Before she could open her mouth to speak, he cupped the back of her neck and pinned his gaze to hers. "Are you hurt anywhere?"

"N-no," she managed, licking her lips to ease the dryness.

"You sure?"

She realized his fingers were resting against the pulse beating below the angle of her jaw. "Yes." She was shaking for a different reason now, the relief overwhelming. But there was something even more crucial she had to tell him. "Xang said this isn't the primary target," she blurted.

He stopped what he was doing and she craned her neck around to locate the team leader. He was out in the hallway, still holding the grenade. "I overheard Xang talking to the other men," she continued in a rush. "He said something about us being a distraction, that this wasn't the real target."

Jake stiffened. She knew the team leader had heard her because he let out a curse and started reporting everything to someone via his earpiece.

She looked back at Jake. "They shot Celida—"

"I heard," he said, voice grim. "Do you know where Xang is now?" He cut away the tape holding her lower legs to the chair.

She shook her head, struggling not to cry as he freed her. She'd been so sure she'd die in here. "He was here when they taped the grenade to me then they all left together, but—"

"Okay. Come on." He didn't ask whether she could walk or not, simply scooped her up and started carrying her for the door.

"Wait!"

"Your brother's fine. Schroder's got him and he's a former PJ."

She didn't know what a PJ was but this wasn't the time to ask.

Jake started walking again. He was two strides from the doorway when a large explosion rumbled up through the floor beneath them.

Jake froze and immediately went down on one knee, hunching over her in a protective move that made her want to cry more.

"We just had an explosion somewhere below us," she heard the team leader report. "Can you confirm?" A pause. "Copy that."

He spoke more loudly as he addressed the team. "Bomb the EOD team hadn't gotten to yet just detonated. Assume the entire east side of the floor two floors down is gone. Execute exfil plan delta. Let's move it."

"How confident are they that they've found all the other devices?" Bauer asked as he came abreast of her and Jake.

"Didn't ask, but assume they haven't," the team leader responded. "We'll check the status of the west staircase."

KAYLEA CROSS

The hallway was just as dark as the room where she'd been held prisoner. Rachel tightened her arms around Jake's neck. "I can walk," she offered.

He grunted. "Nope. No telling what kind of debris we're gonna run across and you don't have shoes on."

She noticed more men lined up further down the hallway and realized there must be a second team. Jake hustled her in line with the others, someone else behind them carrying Brandon. They walked the full length of the hallway to the other side. The lead man in the other team checked the door and rushed through it, his teammates covering his movements.

"Clear."

They descended the steps, curling down and around to the next floor. And that's when she first noticed it.

Smoke.

The man in front held up a raised fist and everyone stopped.

"Alpha squad, go," the team leader commanded. The forward team broke away and went down to investigate. In the few seconds they were gone, the smoke intensified. Jake shifted his hold on her, waiting, and moments later the squad reappeared.

"Fire's almost at the stairwell. Can't tell how far down it goes."

Rachel turned her head to watch the team leader, her stomach cramping at the thought of them having to run the gauntlet of smoke and flame waiting below. But what other choice did they have? No firefighters were getting all the way up here to put the fire out in time.

"Copy that," he answered, then reached up and tapped his earpiece. "This is Charlie one, requesting an emergency rooftop pickup. Advise."

She didn't hear the response, but Jake must have because he turned and immediately started back up the steps as the others did the same.

His foot had just hit the third stair from the top when the door below them crashed open. Everyone froze, dropping to one knee. Rachel drew her knees up and held her breath, heart thudding. Uneven footsteps echoed from down below, then stopped. A loud, hacking cough followed, along with a thickening cloud of smoke.

The team member at the bottom of the stairs had his rifle up, his body absolutely still as he waited. The leader gave him the signal to check the situation and he slowly crept to the next stair, two men right behind him for backup. They'd barely gotten into place before a gunshot rang out and a bullet buried itself into the concrete wall ahead of them.

Instantly everyone hit the floor, Jake rolling her beneath him on the stairs to protect her as the shooter opened fire.

****

Xang pulled the trigger once more and paused, trying to hear whoever was above him, but it was impossible. The blast had blown out his eardrums.

Everything was muffled, like he was underwater, and he had blood coming out of his ears. When it had gone off he'd been sure he was dead, but then he'd come to and pulled himself out of the pile of debris that had fallen around him. His chest hurt too. It felt like something was slicing into him each time he breathed or moved. He wiped distractedly at his stinging, watering eyes with his sleeve, but it didn't help.

He knew whoever was above him had to be law enforcement. Already the smoke was too thick back in the hallway, the heat of the fire making it unbearable. He couldn't go lower because the fire was too intense, so the only option was to go up, even if he didn't know what he'd do once he got there.

But now others stood in his way. The cell had already left him to die—had purposely trapped him in here by detonating that bomb before he managed to get out—and he'd be damned if he was going to let the cops or Feds take him in.

His hand shook as he held the pistol, still aimed up the staircase. No one had returned fire yet. Had he hit them? Or maybe they hadn't been armed at all?

He raised his bleeding left arm to cover his mouth when he coughed again, his throat and lungs already burning from the smoke. His whole body trembled, his breaths choppy and uneven due to his racing heart.

A frantic glance behind him showed the thick, acrid smoke seeping from beneath the bottom of the steel door. He could feel the heat radiating from it. There was no way he could go back in there. The door would buy him some time, but eventually the smoke would overcome him. If he wanted the chance to live he was going to have to make it past whoever was up there and get onto the roof.

Taking a cautious step, he eased his weight forward, trying to get a glimpse up the staircase. The red laser dot on the wall ahead of him stopped him cold. He jerked back, yanked his weapon up and started firing.

Chapter Fifteen

Jake silently cursed and pressed harder against Rachel's back, trying to cover as much of her as possible. Three rapid shots rang out. He heard them impact on the wall and stairs, spraying bits of concrete.

Another shot pinged off the steel railing next to him and glanced past. The guys below him could easily engage and take the shooter out, but command wanted him taken alive for questioning. They needed to find out where the main bomb attack was unfolding and stop it.

The shots stopped. Jake raised his head and rolled off Rachel, keeping his body between her and the shooter. He wasn't really worried about getting shot—he'd gladly take a bullet for her or anyone on his team, but his body armor afforded him a lot more protection than Rachel.

"Take her," he whispered to the guy behind him, who in turn grabbed her under the arms and hauled her up, passing her to the next man in line.

"Evers, you move in and take Ciprioni's place. I want that guy taken alive," the team leader said, his voice quiet in Jake's earpiece.

Without responding verbally Jake rose to a crouch and moved down the stairs to take Ciprioni's position behind Bauer. Jake couldn't see anything past the big bastard's shoulders, but he placed a hand on the left one to alert Bauer that he was in position and ready to rock.

In a fluid rush, Bauer started down the steps. The shooter got off another round that buried itself in the wall over their heads.

"Freeze!" Bauer shouted. Jake caught a flash of movement from down below and Bauer squeezed off one shot. A sharp cry of pain followed, then a clatter as the shooter dropped his weapon.

Jake was right on Bauer's heels as they reached the bottom of the stairs and made the turn, rifles aimed on the man writhing on the concrete floor. Smoke billowed up from under the steel door behind him but as he turned over Jake was able to get a good look at him.

"It's Xang," he growled to the others. Fucker was bleeding from a wound high up in his shoulder, which was no accident.

Bauer would have put two rounds in the guy's chest and another in his head if the orders had been different. Jake wanted to tear the bastard apart for what he'd done to Rachel and her brother. Reining that primal urge in, he locked his emotions down as they approached Xang.

Before they could reach him to cuff him and take him into custody, Xang twisted to the side and made a desperate grab for his weapon. Jake launched himself at him.

His shoulder caught Xang in the chest an instant before they slammed into the ground, the impact and Jake's weight knocking the breath out of Xang. Jake got to his knees and straddled him, flipping him over onto his belly so he could wrench his arms behind his back. Jake wanted the asshole to pay for what he'd done—to rot in prison after he spilled everything he knew about the ongoing terror plot and the cell in general.

Xang screamed and started shouting things Jake

couldn't understand. Jake ignored him, getting the flex cuffs on tight before hauling Xang to his feet and bodily shoving him up the stairs. Bauer grabbed Xang under one arm and together they dragged him kicking and twisting up to the door at the top. The rest of the team was already filing out, taking Rachel and Brandon with them onto the roof.

Now they waited for their ride to show up. The entire team, two civilians, one hostage and a live grenade.

Jake and Bauer forced Xang through the doorway into the bright April sunshine. A stiff, cool wind blew but Jake didn't feel it, too amped up on adrenaline to feel anything but a sense of vindication as they dragged the prisoner over to the team leader and dumped him face down.

The team leader raised his eyebrows at them. "All clear?"

"Yessir," they both answered.

"Then I'm gonna get rid of this," he said, holding up the grenade.

Jake stood back. No way anyone from the EOD was gonna make it up to take care of that for them, and they sure as hell couldn't take it on board the bird. The team leader paused at the steel door a second before lobbing the thing down the stairs and slamming the door shut.

"Fire in the hole!" the team leader yelled, crouching down away from the door as the rest of the team did the same. Seconds later a loud thud shook the ground. Problem solved.

Schroder trotted over to start administering first aid, and the moment he turned Xang over, Jake heard the guy curse.

"I'll slow the bleeding but this could be touch and go," he muttered as he wrenched Xang's shirt away.

The wound in his shoulder had torn a chunk of flesh

away, exposing the bone, but that wasn't the worst part. Something—either a bullet fragment or a piece of shrapnel from the explosion had buried itself in Xang's chest. A rivulet of blood trickled from it but now Jake realized it wasn't just the smoke causing Xang to cough. Pink froth came from his nose and mouth as he hacked away, gasping for breath as it eased. His lung had been damaged.

"Birds are nine minutes out," the team leader informed them.

Jake glanced over at Rachel. One of the guys was giving her some water while another tended to Brandon's injured hand. Guy looked pale and listless but Rachel was alert and coherent. She looked over at him, met his gaze, and gave him a wobbly smile.

That's my girl, he thought, smiling in return.

"Stop making eyes at your woman and fucking help me here," Schroder muttered, digging in his med kit for something to staunch the bleeding with.

Jake tore clothing out of the way and applied pressure to the wound in Xang's ruined shoulder as the former PJ worked. Right at the designated time the muted thud of rotors sounded in the distance. Jake looked up to find them at his ten o'clock, heading straight to the rooftop. There wasn't enough room for them to both touch down so they'd have to remain in a hover while they loaded one bird, then the other.

The first one came in, hovered above the deck for a few moments before the crew chief on board lowered the Stokes litter. Schroder finished his initial treatment and stood. Jake helped him lift Xang, who was no longer fighting for anything except the ability to breathe, and together they ran him to the bird.

After loading Xang into the litter and hoisting him inside, the crew winched the others aboard. Safely inside the belly of the helo, Jake glanced back. Rachel was still across the rooftop with her brother and the rest of the guys, waiting for the second helo.

The team leader gave the signal to the pilots and the Blackhawk lifted off. Schroder was back working on Xang, who didn't look good at all. Bastard deserved every millisecond of pain he suffered, but death would be way too fucking easy. Jake was just glad that Xang wasn't on the same helo as Rachel so she wouldn't have to see him again.

They climbed and banked slightly to the left and Jake looked out the open door. Rachel was crouched with another team member, waiting to run to the second helo that had just moved into its final hover position. She glanced up at his bird and shaded her eyes.

Unsure if she could see him he waved, his heart squeezing when she waved back then turned and ran for the second Hawk. As his helo flew away he saw the second lift off and carry the others away from the burning building.

Jake leaned his head back and closed his eyes, thanking God that Rachel was going to be okay. If she'd let him, he was going to spend the rest of his life making sure she never had anything to fear ever again. And he would make sure she knew it as soon as this was all over.

****

The antiseptic and slightly stale smell of the hospital had long since faded from Rachel's notice. She paused at Brandon's bedside to gaze down at his sleeping form. He was pale, dehydrated and exhausted, but the surgeons had cleaned up the amputation site and the IV fluids would help him recover quickly.

Physically at least. Mentally and emotionally could be a different story.

Since the nurses had told her he'd be sleeping for the next while at least, Rachel gently brushed her fingers over his forehead and eased the door shut behind her. It took a few minutes to navigate her way through the surgical ward to the elevators and find the neurological ward.

Stepping off the elevator she headed past the nurse's station and down the hall. She saw right away where the room was because Agent Travers was standing outside it.

He nodded when he saw her. "How's your brother?" he asked when she got close.

"Sleeping." But safe, and that's all that mattered. She glanced at the window in the door. "How is she?"

"Pissed."

Rachel blinked and looked at him. "About the attack?"

"No, mostly that she didn't drop the two bastards who came after you. She'll be glad to see you though. I didn't tell her you were here."

"Can I go in?"

"Sure." He held the door open and allowed her to enter first.

Celida was propped up in her hospital bed with two pillows behind her bandaged head, and even with both eyes swollen and turning black and blue, Rachel could tell she was scowling. Another bandage covered her right cheek, stark against her caramel skin. The woman's expression transformed into one of relief the instant she saw Rachel through her slitted eyes. "You are such a sight for sore eyes."

"I'm glad, but they do look pretty sore all right," Rachel answered, halting at her bedside. God, her face looked awful. "Are you... Can I get you anything?"

Celida waved a hand and Rachel noticed that her other forearm was bandaged. "I'm fine. Just banged up a bit. And this one on my face is just gonna make me look more badass when the stitches come out." She gestured to the jagged row of stitches closing the wound on her right cheek, eyed Rachel as best she could through all the swelling. "What about you?"

"I'm not hurt. I consider that a major miracle." Scrapes, bumps and bruises were nothing. Those hours she'd spent strapped to that chair with the grenade in her hands had been the longest of her life. "You should have seen the guys in action when they came in to rescue us," she said with an awed shake of her head. "It was just like in the movies, except it was happening to me."

The corner of Celida's mouth turned up in a half-smile. "Yeah, those guys are badass."

Almost shyly, she reached for Rachel's hand. Rachel wrapped her fingers around Celida's and returned the pressure when she squeezed. "I'm so glad you're okay. When they got through the door I thought…" She lowered her gaze as though guilt-stricken that she hadn't stopped them.

"God, no, and don't you ever blame yourself for what happened," Rachel said urgently, squeezing her hand harder. "They freaking shot you and bashed you in the head, so you can't possibly blame yourself, okay?"

Celida shrugged, the set of her jaw telling Rachel that she didn't agree. "Was Jake there?"

"Yeah. He was in the entry team and was the one to take the grenade off my hands." She wrapped her arms around herself and staved off a shudder at the memory. "I'm not an idiot—I know what he does on the job, but seeing him in action was an eye-opening experience. He was so calm and in control the whole time." She glanced at Travers, unsure of how much she could reveal, even though she knew Celida must have all kinds of security clearance for this case.

"Go ahead, she's gonna find out everything when

she gets outta here anyway," the man said.

"Well, he and Bauer brought down Xang, too," she continued. "I was terrified when I realized he was heading down the stairwell to get him but it was all over in under a minute."

"That's why those guys are the best in the business," Celida murmured. Her gaze shifted to Travers. "Any word on Tucker? I think he came up to see me before the medics transported me from the hotel." She frowned as though she couldn't quite remember, which Rachel thought was understandable considering the concussion and shock she must have been in.

"His team's been deployed to the primary target," he said. "Xang gave everything up once they stabilized him on the way back to base. They'd also planted bombs at the Chinese consulate. EOD teams have locked it down as well as the hotel and all the dignitaries have been evacuated with the rest of the guests. If the devices go off, at least no one's inside anymore. And we've got some great leads on the two cell members who attacked you guys. Teams are out hunting them now, so it shouldn't be long until they're dealt with."

"That's good to hear," Celida murmured.

"He asked me to get you this, by the way." Travers dug in his pocket and pulled out a caramel-filled candy bar. "He said it's your favorite."

Celida took it. "It is," she said with a little smile. Rachel was surprised to see the female agent blink fast as though fighting tears, and she was desperately curious about the history between those two. Clearly they were both into each other. And she was glad that the gesture had managed to put a real smile on Celida's face. That told her all she needed to know about the woman's feelings for him.

"So, you ready to get out of here and take care of

the reports now?" Travers asked Rachel.

She withheld a groan at the thought of answering more questions and filling out paperwork when all she wanted to do was see Jake and sleep for the next two days. "Sure." She set a hand on Celida's shoulder. "I'll come visit you tomorrow."

"Nah, they're discharging me in the morning. Just want to keep me overnight for observation, blah blah."

"Well then I'll call you."

Her lips quirked. "Do that. Maybe I can meet up with you and Jake for dinner or something sometime."

"Sounds great." Though she didn't know when she'd see him next. Travers had told her Jake was back at base doing after-action reports and debriefings, so she didn't expect to see him for the next day or two at least, though she was sure he'd call her when he could. She followed Travers out into the hallway. "Where am I going after the paperwork?" she asked him.

A small smile curved his mouth. "Up to you, but Jake already asked me to take you to his place once we're done. Unless you have somewhere else in mind."

"No, that sounds good." Really good. And now she just wanted this damn paperwork done with so she could be at his place when he got home. Having looked death in the eye today she'd made up her mind not to hold anything back from Jake. She knew what she wanted— him in her life forever. She just hoped he wanted the same.

Chapter Sixteen

Jake's heart was pounding as he parked his truck in his driveway. The house sat dark and silent in front of him but all he could think about was that Rachel was in there. He'd showered and changed as fast as he could at HQ, then raced to get home.

Travers had texted him hours ago to say he'd dropped Rachel off. With Xang in custody—in a shitload of pain, which he considered fucking awesome—and the two cell members who had attacked Rachel and Celida in the hotel dead during a shootout with Tuck's squad, she'd been perfectly safe alone here. He knew Travers had offered to stay to keep her company in case she didn't feel comfortable being alone, but she'd turned him down so they'd placed a couple unmarked cars on the perimeter just in case.

Tuck had seen Jake back at Quantico after the op and debriefings, and after telling him Rachel was staying at their place Tuck had offered to crash elsewhere to give them some much needed privacy. Jake was grateful because the way he felt right now, he wasn't going to be able to tone down his response when he saw her.

His hands actually shook a little as he slid the key into the front lock. Fuck, all night long he'd been thinking about her, agonizing about not being with her. From the moment his helo had flown to a secret CIA holding facility to unload their prisoner, he'd run through everything that had happened over and over again.

But now the threat was over. All the bombs at the primary hotel had been located and rendered inert. The fire at the initial hotel was out. Civilian casualties were minimal and minor, and every single man on the team had come back to base in one piece.

Now it was time for him and Rachel to discuss their relationship going forward.

Right after he got her naked, drove as deep as he could get inside her and made her come until she was too sated to move.

His body was tight as a wire, his cock already hard at the thought. There'd be plenty of time to talk afterward—right now he needed to claim her, mark her on the most primal level. He didn't care if it was Neanderthal as shit; he just knew he needed to be inside her in the next ten minutes or he'd die.

The alarm beeped softly when he cracked the door open. After disarming it, he closed the door behind him, locked it and looked around as he took his boots off. There were no lights on and he didn't hear anything. Was Rachel already upstairs asleep? The thought of crawling in beside her and waking her with a series of slow, damp kisses up the length of her naked spine made his cock swell against his fly.

He'd just set his foot on the bottom tread of the stairs to the second floor when he heard a movement behind him. He turned to see Rachel standing in the living room doorway, her hair loose around her shoulders, dressed in one of his T-shirts that hung to just above her knees.

"Hi," she said softly, smiling at him.

His heart squeezed so tight it seemed to stop beating for a second.

Rather than respond, he erased the distance between them with a few quick strides and grabbed her up in his arms. She let out a deep exhalation and hugged him back. Jake buried his face in the silky mass of her hair. She smelled of his soap, was dressed in his shirt. He couldn't fucking wait to get her up in his bed, in his sheets and imprint the feel and scent of him all over her.

"I missed you," she whispered, kissing his temple.

"I bet I missed you more," he argued, savoring every single point of contact between them. He was acutely aware of the way her trim curves molded to him, her breasts cushioned against his chest and that she was bare-ass naked beneath that T-shirt.

Unable to take it a second longer, Jake cupped the back of her head and claimed her mouth. Rachel made a murmuring sound and parted her lips for the thrust of his tongue. Like a spark to dry tinder, he caught fire. Flames raced over his skin and the only one who could extinguish them was her.

Jake twisted them around and pinned her up against the door, trapping her between the hard surface and his body. A throaty moan answered him and she rolled her hips against him. His clothes were suddenly irritating the shit out of his skin.

Keeping her in place with his hips and one hand between her shoulder blades to protect her from the hard door, he reached his free hand up, grabbed a fistful of cotton and wrenched his shirt over his head. It landed on the floor somewhere behind him but all he could focus on was Rachel and the molten hot look in her eyes as she pulled her own shirt off. Holding her naked body, drinking in the sight and scent of her, Jake growled at the way her hard nipples tightened and her parted sex pressed so provocatively against his covered erection.

Grabbing a fistful of her hair, he crushed his mouth over hers, half frantic to get inside her. He turned them again and made for the stairs, stopping once partway up because he was so distracted by the feel of those hard little nipples rubbing against his skin. He bent his head to take one hard point into his mouth, sucked with a firm pressure and reveled in her whimper as she ground her groin into the covered bulge of his cock.

Somehow he got them up the stairs without tripping and into his bedroom. His wide king-size bed lay in the center of the far wall.

He carried her there, wrenched the quilt back and laid her out. A territorial thrill shot through him at the sight of her there, stretched out naked on her back like an offering, her eyes glinting with pure need as she stared up at him. With his crazy schedule and the kind of work he did he rarely brought a woman back to his place, and never since he'd moved in with Tuck. He was glad Rachel was the first. This was everything he'd fantasized about come true.

He stripped off his jeans, underwear and socks and climbed over top of her. Rachel wound those silken arms around his back, her hands stroking his overheated skin. She raised her head as he lowered his weight onto her, and moaned into his mouth. Jake kissed her hard and deep, twining his tongue with hers. She was so fucking soft and warm and all his.

"Jake, get inside me. Now," she panted, arching against him.

He was too worked up to slow down now and give her the foreplay she deserved. He'd make it up to her a thousand times over later on. Leaning his weight on one elbow, he yanked the bedside table drawer open and got a condom. This time when he came he wanted to be buried as deep inside her as he could get and feel every pulse of her sex around him. When he rose to his knees and tore the packet open, she surprised him by wrapping her slender fingers around his throbbing cock and taking the condom from him.

He shuddered and bit back a groan as she rolled it down the sensitive shaft, inch by torturous inch. Then she reached up to tangle her hands in his hair and wrapped her legs around his hips, pressing her open folds to his aching cock.

"Get inside me," she begged, undulating beneath him.

Fuck. He couldn't wait anymore.

He levered up on one hand and fitted the crown of his cock against her soft folds. His muscles were knotted up, his breathing as unsteady as his pulse. He paused only long enough to look down into Rachel's eyes. They were half-closed, dreamy and yet full of anticipation. And he couldn't hold off another goddamn second.

Gripping her hip to hold her steady, he pushed, sliding deep until every inch of his cock was buried inside her. She was so tight and wet, her inner walls rippling around him. Sparks of ecstasy raced up his spine. Helpless against the lash of pleasure, he closed his eyes and moaned as he leaned forward to press his face into the side of her neck, a shudder ripping through him.

Slick. Soft.

Perfect.

In the shower it had been good, but here in the comfort of his bed where they could slow down and savor each other, it was fucking amazing. He was surrounded by her, enfolded by her heat and softness, her hold on him surprisingly strong.

"Jake…"

Her breathy moan penetrated the fog of lust, but just barely. Not wanting to be a completely selfish bastard, he began to move, starting out in a slow, steady rhythm. He used her sighs and gasps to gauge his movements, making sure to add a little circular motion at the end of the in-stroke to rub his body against her clit.

"Oh! Do that again…"

He repeated the movement. "This?"

A loud whimper answered him, her slick inner muscles squeezing around him. "*Yes*." Her voice was tight, desperate.

Any fucking time you want, babe.

He gritted his teeth against the need to come, the pleasure already climbing to the critical point. Beneath him Rachel rocked in time to his thrusts, the pressure of her fingers in his back and her heels in his ass silently begging him for more. Demanding it.

He let his tightly held control go a little, increasing the force of his thrusts. Her moans, the breathless little cries that echoed through the room drove him into a frenzy. He drove deep, hard. Soon she was clinging, crying out in desperation as he pounded into her. The headboard thudded against the wall and the bed shook. She was right there with him, straining and writhing in his grip, trying to get him closer, deeper.

His tongue trailed a damp path down the side of her neck to where it curved into her shoulder. Rachel clutched at him, circling her hips and a wild cry broke free from her lips. He felt her sex contract around him, felt the rhythmic pulses as she milked his cock and sobbed in ecstasy. Her release undid him. His hips jackhammered, his body on auto-pilot as the need took over.

"*Rachel*," he gasped out, lost in her and what she was making him feel. Nothing had ever felt like this.

The orgasm rushed at him, filling every cell before it peaked and held, wringing out his release as his muscles shook and he groaned like a dying man. Through it all Rachel cradled him to her, holding him close as it finally faded, her fingers drifting through his hair, over his shoulders and down his back.

"I love you."

At the whispered words he managed to lift his head, surprised that she'd been the first one to say it because he'd been planning to. Her eyes were dreamy, her expression contented. It made him feel ten feet tall to know he'd put that look on her face, to know he'd finally won her love. "I love you too."

She gave him a supremely satisfied smile and leaned up to place a kiss so tender on his lips that it made his chest ache. "I thought you might. But it's nice to know for sure."

"Babe, just gimme the chance to show you how much."

"Pretty sure I saw that earlier today. And just now."

Christ, every time he thought about entering that room and seeing her tied with that grenade in her hands, he broke out in a cold sweat. "No one's ever gonna hurt you or scare you like that again. I promise."

She kissed the tip of his nose. "I believe you. And thanks for saving me today."

Jake cupped her face in his hands and stared down into her eyes. "You were so brave, sweetheart."

It floored him to think of how resilient she was, that core of inner strength untouched by all she'd faced in the past few days. Which was good, because girlfriends and wives of guys in law enforcement had to be tough, to cope with the stress and high tempo of the job, or everything would fall apart. He'd been through a relationship like that already but he knew Rachel could handle it. And he had every intention of making her his wife someday.

She snorted softly. "I felt a whole lot braver after you showed up, trust me."

"Good. Because from now on you'll always have me to back you up." Whatever came at her, he'd be standing at her side, and in front of her when she needed him to shield her.

She flashed him another soft smile that twisted him up inside. The woman was incredible. Gentle, serene, yet incredibly tough, all wrapped up in an elegant package. He knew she'd always take his breath away whenever she walked into a room. "That sure sounds like you're thinking long term, Mr. Evers."

"Why yes, I am, Miss Granger. Very long term. I've already waited for you my whole life. I don't want to go without you anymore." He stroked a thumb over her cheekbone, marveling at how delicate she seemed when in reality she was one of the strongest people he knew. "I want you to move in with me. We'll find a place you like. I want you next to me when I fall asleep in our bed and have you there when I wake up."

A light sheen of moisture filled her eyes. "I'd love that."

"Good. We'll start looking for places tomorrow." And not long after they moved in together, he wanted a ring on her finger as a symbol of his commitment to her, and show the world she was his.

Rachel laughed softly and drew him down once more, surrounding him with her embrace and her love. "Sounds like a plan."

Epilogue

Six weeks later

Rachel shifted her briefcase to her left hand and inserted the key into the lock on the condo door with her right. After a long week filled with overtime while trying to meet deadlines on an upcoming project, she was looking forward to a quiet night of unwinding with a glass or two of red wine.

Slipping inside, the sound of male voices reached her.

She smiled in anticipation, slipped off her shoes and set her briefcase on the kitchen island. A wine glass was waiting for her near the edge, already filled with a few inches of garnet deliciousness. The sight warmed her inside. "I'm home."

"Hey, we're back here," Jake called out. "Have a good day?"

"Long."

Picking up her wine, she reached up to pull the clip from her hair and let it fall around her shoulders. Jake loved it when she wore her hair loose and she had every intention of using every seductive weapon in her arsenal tonight. Yeah, she was tired, but she wasn't *dead*, and there was no way she could be in the same room with Jake and not want him. Besides, spending a quiet Friday night with him at home was rare with his crazy work and training schedule, so she was determined to make the most of it.

She strode through the kitchen, her feet nearly silent on the hardwood floors, and into the living room. Jake half-turned around on the leather couch to look at her, his smile of welcome making everything right with her world.

She loved coming home to this place they'd moved into over a month ago. Out the wall-to-wall windows on the south side of the condo they had a gorgeous view of the DC skyline, the sky already turning a soft purple as the stars winked to life one by one.

Not that either of them was paying the slightest attention to the view. Brandon was on the loveseat opposite the unlit fireplace, a baseball game displayed on the large flat screen TV—Jake was *such* a guy, and as much as she loathed how much of the living room wall space the thing took up, she'd merely rolled her eyes when he'd bought it, knowing how crucial its presence was for him to feel at home in their new place.

He'd let her do whatever she wanted pretty much everywhere else in the condo, other than all his military and law enforcement awards and paraphernalia he displayed in their home office, so she couldn't complain. She'd been careful to keep the colors light and neutral, the furniture a bit masculine, the overall look soothing. He'd told her how much he loved coming home and it pleased her to know she'd created a tranquil home where he could recharge after the long days he put in.

"Hi," she murmured, leaning over the back of the couch to kiss Jake. She was careful to lean far enough over to give him an eyeful of her cleavage and the lacy black push-up bra she wore beneath her red silk sheath.

"Hi yourself," he murmured back, his heated gaze dipping down right where she'd known it would go.

He was so easy, but she knew she'd never tire of him wanting her so much. Usually they didn't get to fall asleep together often throughout the week and he travelled a lot for trainings, but when he was home he more than made up for his absence with lots of hot loving. Many times over the past six weeks he'd come home in the middle of the night and woken her by crawling naked into bed beside her, rousing her from sleep with heated kisses and caresses that led to even hotter, more delicious things. He'd already made it abundantly clear that he intended to marry her someday, and she was so on board with that plan.

Rounding the couch, she cradled her wineglass in one hand and lowered herself beside Jake, who stretched out an arm to wrap around her as he drew her into the curve of his body. His scent and the feel of his muscular frame pressed to her back filled her with longing. She leaned her head back against his shoulder and closed her eyes with a heartfelt sigh of contentment when he kissed the top of her head.

"You two are brutal at making me feel like a fifth wheel all the time," Brandon muttered, shaking his head in disgust as he focused on the ballgame.

"Tough," Rachel said with a satisfied smile. She opened her eyes and looked over at him, all comfy on the loveseat. "How did your appointment go?"

He held up his hand, which no longer sported a bandage. "They're upping my physio appointments to four times a week, but I think so far they're pleased with my progress. I think the receptionist has a thing for me. And she's way hot."

She chuckled. "Well, that's good, I guess."

He slung his head around to look at her. "Yeah, so maybe from now on I'll be spending my Friday and

Saturday nights with her instead of here being bothered by all the hot and heavy vibes you guys give off all the time."

Jake's chest moved as he smothered a laugh. "Sorry, pal. Can't help it with her."

Brandon shrugged. "Whatever. I know how it is when things are new, the whole infatuation-slash-honeymoon phase. But she's my sister, man. It's gross."

"I don't think she's gross," Jake murmured, one hand playing with her hair as he nuzzled the side of her neck in a way he knew was guaranteed to make her shiver.

"Ugh, can't you at least wait until the game's over and then I'll go to bed so you guys can...whatever?" He shifted on the loveseat, practically squirming in discomfort.

She felt Jake smile against her neck. "Cope, Brandon," she told him. "Just watch the game and ignore us."

"Believe me, I'm trying," he muttered.

She loved the banter between them. Just like old times. Brandon was healing fast, both physically and emotionally, and her now twice weekly counseling appointments were helping her deal with everything that had happened. But then, nothing was as good as falling asleep and waking up in Jake's arms, or at least hearing his voice over the phone every day. He still had to travel for training or exercises sometimes but so far he hadn't been out on another op since the kidnapping.

In other good news, Celida was all healed up now—well, physically anyway. Rachel had talked to her a few times on the phone and when Tuck had last been over a week ago he'd told her that Celida was doing fine and about to start work again this coming Monday.

As for Tuck, the man was dealing with a lot of stressful personal crap right now, and adjusting to a new roommate who wasn't exactly made of sunshine and rainbows. Though Jake still owned half the house he and Tuck had bought together, Bauer had moved in there a month ago. His rent went toward utilities and property taxes so Jake wouldn't have to pay that on top of what he already did for their new place. Rachel had only seen Bauer a couple of times since then but despite his grim, often aloof manner, he and Tuck seemed to share a roof well enough.

"By the way, I've got the day off tomorrow," Jake murmured against her skin.

That got her attention. "You do?"

"Yep. So unless something goes sideways, I'm all yours until Sunday morning."

Ooh, the possibilities…

He chuckled as if he knew what she was thinking, the warmth of his breath tickling her. "Thought I could take you to the range for your first lesson."

She twisted around to look at him. "Really?"

"You up for it?"

She beamed at him, already looking forward to it. "Totally up for it. And then lunch and maybe a rappelling lesson after?"

His white teeth flashed in the midst of his dark stubble as he grinned, little crow's feet fanning out from his eyes. "Love the enthusiasm, but one thing at a time, babe."

She turned back around to face the TV. "Yeah, guess I have to be careful not to wear you out on your day off." Her comment got her a grunt and a tickle in the ribs.

For a while she lay there basking in the cozy atmosphere, but she quickly bored of watching the game. "Your team's losing by six runs in the fifth inning," she finally said to Jake. "You really want to keep watching?"

"I guess I could be persuaded to stop," he

whispered, his voice taking on that seductive edge that made her all shivery with anticipation. "What should we do instead?"

Brandon made a strangled sound and shifted again on the loveseat.

Rachel bit back a laugh. Taking pity on him, she rose and tugged Jake to his feet. "G'night, Brandon."

"G'night."

She headed for the master bedroom, her entire body humming with the awareness that Jake was right behind her. She heard Brandon turn the volume on the game way up. Presumably to drown out any psychologically scarring sounds he was afraid he might hear.

Turning to circle her arms around Jake's neck, she raised up on tiptoe to kiss him as he walked her backward into the room and closed the door with a firm click, locking out the world for the rest of the night. The sound had barely registered before his hands got busy stripping her out of her work clothes, his mouth slanted across hers as he deepened the kiss, his erection hard against her belly.

"Mmmm," she murmured into his mouth, heat exploding low in her abdomen. Suddenly impatient, she broke this kiss long enough to grab the hem of his T-shirt and yank it over his head, flinging it to the floor. With a low growl Jake fisted a hand in her hair and brought his mouth down on hers, a primal, possessive claiming. She shivered at the thought of what was coming. Fast this time. Hard. Then later, soft and slow, taking the time to explore and tease to their hearts' content.

And the night was still very young.

As Jake lowered her onto their king-sized bed, Rachel gazed up into his heated stare and smiled in anticipation, her body alive with tingles. A whole night and an entire day off with Jake. She was going to make the most of every single moment she had him all to herself.

—The End—

Complete Booklist

Romantic Suspense
Hostage Rescue Team Series
Marked

Titanium Security Series
Ignited
Singed
Burned
Extinguished
Rekindled

Bagram Special Ops Series
Deadly Descent
Tactical Strike
Lethal Pursuit
Danger Close

Suspense Series
Out of Her League
Cover of Darkness
No Turning Back
Relentless
Absolution

Paranormal Romance
Empowered Series
Darkest Caress

Historical Romance
The Vacant Chair

Erotic Romance (writing as ***Callie Croix***)
Deacon's Touch
Dillon's Claim
No Holds Barred
Touch Me
Let Me In
Covert Seduction

Acknowledgements

A big shout out to my readers, who demanded a story for Jake. Thanks so much for your support!

As always, to my long-suffering critique partner, Katie Reus, who has to listen to me whine whenever I hit a wall with the storyline of whatever book I'm working on at the time.

Julieanne Reeves, you left this world far too soon and you will be missed greatly by those of us who got to know you. If the world was filled with people as warm and supportive as you, it would be a much better place to live in.

Todd, you're the best proofer a gal could ask for, plus you work for cheap, which is AWESOME, so thank you.

And last but not least, to Joan, my editor who I met at RT in New Orleans this year, a big squishy hug. Thank you for your eagle eye!

About the Author

NY Times and USA Today Bestselling author Kaylea Cross writes edge-of-your-seat military romantic suspense. Her work has won many awards and has been nominated for both the Daphne du Maurier and the National Readers' Choice Awards. A Registered Massage Therapist by trade, Kaylea is also an avid gardener, artist, Civil War buff, Special Ops aficionado, belly dance enthusiast and former nationally-carded softball pitcher. She lives in Vancouver, BC with her husband and family.

You can visit Kaylea at www.kayleacross.com. If you would like to be notified of future releases, please join her newsletter: http://kayleacross.com/v2/contact/

6912186R00132

Printed in Great Britain
by Amazon.co.uk, Ltd.,
Marston Gate.